Love, Trust and Loyalty

LOVE, TRUST AND LOYALTY

First edition. February 14, 2023.

Copyright © 2023 Karen Renee.

ISBN: 979-8215810866

Written by Karen Renee.

This book is dedicated to learning how to love, even if the love is you. And the love that inspired me.

Lyne'e Loyalty Riggs

For most of my friends, going to college meant getting out of their city and into something bigger, better and more fun. Our senior year, all my friends could talk about were the parties, ice breakers, games and hangouts in whatever state they were going to attend. By then, there was no such thing as new anything or anybody, yet all anyone could think about was the idea of "new". For me, college wasn't a question, it was a testimony, written on the walls of some ancient ruins in blood, my blood the day I learned to walk. I never even imagined a life where college was not life, hell if I did, I'm sure my mother would come out of nowhere and knock the thought right back into my head like she was hitting a home run when baseball was good during the steroid era.

I have one of *those* mothers. If men are from Mars and women from Venus then my mother is the and me Jupiter. Close enough to know there is warmth, but just too far to feel it. Paulette is perfection, if it's to be done, she's already done it and did it better than anyone foolish enough to come after her. The closest thing to her level of perfection on the face of God's green earth, would have to come from her golden womb. She was never satisfied with anything or anyone, except my sister. In my mom's eyes my sister was the second coming and could spit gold, split atoms with her eyes and if she happened to fart *because ladies don't fart,* that fart would be a rainbow and smell like Channel #5. Me on the other hand, I'm *her other* daughter. I *take after my father*, in fact I heard that so often I could have easily thought that was my actual name. I am second born to a southern bell diva wannabe. No, I'm not ugly, far cry from it, but to my mother, Paulette I just was not pretty enough.

I am the more melanated, thicker, shorter hair *flawed* daughter. It's a burden that I've learned to live with, in fact it's one of the stones or building blocks depending on who's asking that has made me who I am today.

My sister Toni was always in a pageant, program or play, she was my mother's prize possession and her perfect ideal of beauty. Toni was the version of Paulette that even she didn't measure up to. Toni was a constant reassurance to my mother that she was beautiful, how could she not be, look at her daughter. By her sixteenth birthday, Toni was all legs. She stood 5'8 bare foot and weighed 125 pounds soaking wet. Everything about her appearance made her seem magical to me as a child, it's like someone drew her up. She has the most mesmerizing eyes I had ever seen in person. Her eyebrows were naturally long and sharp, they seemed to meet every one of her dark lush eyelashes perfectly. And those eyes, one cat like green and the other an exhaust gray that you couldn't help but stare into every time she allowed them to fall on you. For years I've watched her use those eyes as a weapon of mass destruction, destroying the hearts of poor foolish boys for miles to come or simply the threat of them watering up could bring down an entire empire instantly. She had a cute little upturned nose and plush heart-shaped lips... with tiny little freckles. All of that beauty blended perfectly with warm honey, even skin. For the life of me I could never compete with that type of beauty and freckles.

My mom flaunted her everywhere, she was the center of our family portraits, the first one to walk into a room, the first mentioned in a conversation and then there was me, I was her shadow. "Baby every star shines, but not every star shines as bright as the North Star" consoled by my maternal grandmother every time I was forced to visit with her.

Yes, college was a way out, not just out of this house or city, but this prison.

Anderson and I met freshman year at Texas A&M. He was originally a football jock with a major in business management, but after a few weeks with me his interest quickly changed to finance and analytics. I remember the first day we met; it was a week into our economics class. I wore my favorite pink velour jogging pants with a baby tee and some clean all white Air 1's. For once I was in a place where I wasn't Toni's little sister so I got to dress however I wanted. After years of being uncomfortable and stuffy all I wanted to do was relax and find my rhythm. Anderson sat on the other side of the room in some jeans and an oversized t-shirt. The same basic wardrobe every dude in my school wore, nothing special.

Economics started off with a mock debate, and as president of the debate team back home, this would be an easy A. I began arguing the purchasing power of women in the auto field when Anderson interrupted me with some stupid joke about "chicks vs. cars". He got a few chuckles from other dumbass boys who ride shotgun in their mom cars or on the bus, but not enough to completely distract me from making my point. By the end of class both our professor and I were over his childish ass interruptions and was just ready for the end of lecture.

"If you can take time out of being the teacher's pet today, you should swing by here later." rambled a deep voice from behind me. Anderson dropped a flyer on my books and walked away as I rolled my eyes. For the life of me I don't know what bothered me more, being referred to as a "teacher's pet" *still* or his arrogant demeanor. I mean he didn't even bother to look me in my face, just dropped a damn flyer on me like I was a car windshield and kept moving. *"Fucking gym rats"*

I spent the whole day in a spiral of thoughts, although I worked my ass off to get here, I did not come all of this way to still be called *a teacher's pet* I left that shit back home. And by someone who didn't even know me, yes I answer questions when asked, yes I came prepared, yeah in a full class the professor and I are on a first name basis, but...*shit*.

Later that day, my roommate Sloaneand I went to the hangout. Sloane and I met while taking a tour of the campus my senior year and shared an apartment off campus. The hangout was at what appeared to be Anderson dorm room, there were half dressed girls as far as the eyes can see and guys sweating their every move. It was exactly what I imagined, a room covered in a layer of smoke, chicks of all shapes and sizes in booty shorts and cut up tanks droppin it low and picking it up slow on guys in durags, fake throwback jerseys and baggy jeans. Sloane took no time finding her space in the crowd and leaving me on my own.

"You look lost, Professor McGhee ain't here, if that's who you're waiting on!" Yelled a deep voice so close to my ear that I could feel his lips touching me.

I turned slowly to say something rude, but was quickly distracted by his face. It's a lot more handsome up close. Just as I was getting ready to start my verbal beat down, his alluring, full, nude lips parted displaying a roll of bright white teeth that suddenly began smiling at me. I was stunned for a second, but not a moment longer. "Look, I get it, you must have been the class clown back home and here on some sort of sports scholarship, but the rest of us can't afford to joke our way through class." I snarled, as I snatched my hand out of his hands and turned to walk away. I searched for the door in hopes to escape before my words landed on his dumbass and he understood what I actually said to him, but couldn't find one.

Who the hell does he think he is, he invited me here just to talk shit about me, and what because he's a little cute, I'm supposed to bat my eyes and go along with it.

"So you think I'm a little cute, huh?"

I turn my head a little confused, *can he hear me?* I wondered.

"I must really get under all of that pretty brown skin, if I have you out here talking to yourself?" he asked, as he slowly stepped in my path.

"You really are an arrogant one aren't you?" I questioned stepping my right leg back and taking a long hard look at the man in front of me. He was tall, I'm guessing 6'3 or 6'4, very broad shoulders, thick muscular arms that I could see through his jacket and clearly plays football. You don't get a chest like this sitting around on your ass all day. "You have a room full of adorning females in there, why are you out here tormenting me?" I asked as my eyes made their way back up to his.

"I don't know, maybe out of a room full of adorning females you seem to be the finest one I've seen since stepping on campus". He said while stepping in closer. "I don't want you to leave, but if you are let me walk you back to your dorm?"

"Its fine, I don't stay on campus, anyway. You get back to your party, I'm more than capable of walking home. I reassured him, trying to break his gaze. All of the blood in my body is rushing to my cheeks and I feel nervous energy taking over me. I wanted to stop smiling, but I don't think all the muscles in the world could get my lips to come back together where they belong. From that moment, I was all in. I wanted to be the stuck-up, too good for the boys on campus, pretty girl that was unobtainable, but that shit went out the window ten minutes into a conversation with Anderson Hobbs. I spent the next three weeks learning everything about him, I studied him, his face, his history, his laugh, our future. I even caught myself doodling Lyne'e Hobbs in hearts inside my notebook.

His Bambi-like brown eyes always seem to turn a shade lighter when he spoke of his mom and her smile always made its way into whatever story he told about her. I saw a picture of her once and he was right, her smile could light up a room, I see where he got it from. He has his dad's almond shaped midnight brown eyes and wide nose with his mothers caramel like skin and long lashes. Not a single lump or bump out of place on his entire body and yes I have checked.

We were both from blue-collar families and had to work hard to get here, him on the field and me in the books. The struggle was different, but the struggle was real. I earned a few scholarships, but not enough to completely cover everything.

My dad saved a little for my sister and I to go to college, but of course most of the money went to Toni. She of course didn't need it, she had a full scholarship and pageant money, but my mom insisted that Toni have a car. By the time I was ready for college, there was little left in his savings and even less in my college fund. Between his savings and the scholarships I was able to obtain, I had enough to cover about a third of my tuition, so I worked as a tutor and at a local department store to cover the rest. Staying on campus was also out of the question so I shared an apartment with a friend named Keyla and two other girls. My mother wasn't the open type, well at least not with me. Had it not been for music, movies and my friends over the years I would have never learned about boys, sex and relationships.

Most girls my age and in my situation have their past to draw on, me I have nothing. I watched a relationship between my best friend Aika and this older guy from our neighborhood named Chris. Aika was the closest thing I had to a sister, we shared everything, and I sat shotgun in her relationship. Aika and Chris were the definition of dysfunctional and toxic, but her parent's relationship was as well. The level of toxicity in her house was different from mine, she was the only child and her mother actually liked and loved her. She even brought me along for their Mom and daughter dates, we would go to get mani's and pedi's twice a month and then for dinner. But her dad ended up moving out when we were around thirteen and her mom remarried the next year. Aika started babysitting for a couple down the street and a few months later was in a relationship with the man. Chris was about fifteen years older than us, had a main girl and a baby, but he wanted Aika, and she wanted some attention. I watched him manipulate her mentally, physically and sexually for years. My first real understanding of what sex was, I learned from her.

Paulette told us where babies came from, I wasn't ignorant. I understood what could happen when a man and a woman were intimate and yes I knew how to have sex; I was in high school. It was all anyone of us could really talk about, but no one ever really shared the details. I remember the day Aika and Chris first had sex, her story scared me so bad, after that I was never in a rush to experience it. It was early in the morning before school I understood her story as nonconsensual sex, but she never said it so neither did I.

Her story started off well, he took her to a fancy hotel; he had this enormous dick, and he went down on her, but then tears fell from her eyes. She whispered how painful it was when he just shoved it inside of her. She described what happened next like two dogs during mating season. How she kept trying to adjust or move but he just held her there until he finished. She said he never even looked at her, all of his normal affections and gentleness had gone out the window and when it was over, he left her there bleeding while he went to the bathroom to clean himself off. Just telling me about it made her cry so hard that I cried too. I waited for her to call her experience what it was all day, but the next morning there she was, hopping out of Chris's "97" Sebring Convertible as if nothing had ever happened.

For weeks she would tell me teary-eyed about her sexual experiences with Chris, but she would always go back. He would buy her gifts, give her money, even take us shopping. I would skip school to sit in the clinic with her or be there with her after countless abortions but she just kept going back. The only differences in her stories and some of the other girls in school were the other girls were dealing with age appropriate boys and Aika came with gifts and money. Either way, I had heard enough not to ever want to indulge. Until I met Anderson.

Sex with him was nothing like that, he was gentle with me the first time and every time after. He kissed me softly, he held me after, the only time he was ever possessive or aggressive was during sex when he made me tell him I or "it" was his.

Anderson Hobbs

I used to hate being the baby of the family, it meant that my three older siblings either ignored me or used me. I was the remote, the butler, the practice dummy, the guinea pig, the gopher, the bate, the sacrificial lamb or a combination of all the above. I took shit from everyone on in the house for absolutely everything. I was also the smallest of all my mom's births and the only one born at home. Before it was cool to have a home birth, I was delivered on the living room floor of our home in The Greater Ville hood of St. Louis. We had very little and I made it to college by the skin of my teeth. I earned a partial scholarship to Texas A&M playing football, but on a probationary basis. My grades were alright, but my feet and my hands were going to take me places. I'm lucky enough to come from a two-parent household, and despite how tv and movies portray us, my parents are still together and from what we could tell are still very much in love. My father, William Hobbs Sr. owned a plumbing company while my mother Aretha Hobbs worked at a dental office. In theory they made good money, but for a family with four young children, money was stretched. My dad would pay his last dollar to give us an experience over actual items. He paid for clubs and classes, over name brand clothes and cool toys. We may not have had a lot of the things our friends had, but we went on vacations, family trips and they kept us busy in different activities.

My oldest sister Olivia was clearly the oopp's baby, my momma was sixteen when she had her, later came my brother Will Jr., my sister Ashley and then me Anderson Hobbs. Although I am actually the baby I hate being referred to in that manner.

I have always been my parents most independent and responsible child. No one babied me in that house, I didn't get to throw tantrums, pout, stomp off, there was no running to tell when the older ones were being mean to me, I didn't get away with crap because my parents were over it or just too tired to parent. They taught me to work hard for everything and that ain't shit in life free but failure and that was not an option.

Covering the remainder of my college tuition was a full time job and a lot of sacrifice. Almost everyone we knew chipped in to get me where I am today. My parents were one of the few families to actually own our home so my dad took out a small loan on the house. I worked minor jobs and hustles, my high school teachers took up collections at games, the dentist office my momma worked for made a donation to cover a few of my books. I saved damn near every dollar I made, money that came in from family out of town all went to keep me in school.

Yeah, I wanted to be in the streets with my boys, but my pops made it very clear that I had an opportunity to get out and do something big. He told me all of the time that I had a God given talent and that it was my responsibility to use it. If he saw me slacking off or not working as hard as he felt I should he would be on my ass. I think that's why I've always been the most independent of my siblings. I feel like my dad was harder on me than he was any of the other ones, he never "gave" me anything, I always had to earn the things I wanted. That man and his "lessons" have so much to do with who I am today, a fighter, strong and responsible.

Shit, I was ten years old when I started my first job. Football wasn't even a thought for me, that was my brother's thing. Pop's had me cutting grass around my grandma's neighborhood. There was no such thing as downtime, or time to kick it with my friends. Most of my parent's money went to paying the bills and keeping us afloat, they didn't have money for new shoes and clothes all the time, especially not the clothes and shoes that we wanted. We would get maybe a new outfit or two at the beginning of the school year, but everything else were hand-me-downs or from the church's slightly used bin. So many of my things came from my older brother or even worse, my sisters. Shit, I got into my first fight after showing up to school wearing a pair of my sister's Jordache jeans. Thank God they both got my momma's hips or else not only would the jeans have been too short, but they would have been tight as hell too.

But Will, Will always had something fresh to wear, he got shirts or jackets from his homeboys or at least that's what he would tell our parents whenever he showed up with something new. Will always claimed to have borrowed a pair of shoes or jeans from a friend just to keep my dad from tripping. The truth was, every once in a while he would run an errand for one of the corner boys and they would look out. Or they would throw him some cash on a play or winning game, as a kid I didn't get it, but I learned. Will's shit would be the things you see in video or something, but he was also seven years older than me and played football. Even if I got to sneak out of the house in something of his, they were too big and ended up making me look even worse than I did before. That was until the summer I turned fourteen and finally had a decent growth spurt.

I instantly outgrew all of my siblings and most of my friends in one summer. One day I just woke up in a new body, my feet no longer tiny, they seemed to match the rest of my body. My shoulders were suddenly broad, I had muscles and definition, my back even seemed to have grown. My legs looked as if someone had stretched them out as if they were made of taffy and then wrapped them around a drumstick. All of those features that made me look like my mom, were coming off differently. My little girl lashes were making my big eyes somehow cute. My face as a whole had changed, I didn't experience the grief of hormones the way my sister Ashly did, my skin was smooth and even, my lips were fuller and if you look a little closer, there was hair on my chin. My voice wasn't shaky and scared to come out of my body anymore, just clearing my throat was now a commanding act. I knew the girls were feeling me a little differently than before, but when my mom's friends started talking to me differently I really knew I had changed.

Our neighbor Mr. Decker was a coach at highschool about 20 minutes away, he took one look at me and insisted that I try out for the JV team my freshman year. Even better, he insisted I do it at his highschool. The change in school meant a better curriculum which better my chances at getting into a good college, all the reasons my parents insisted I go.

Football was the best thing that happened to me, I started the year off as Lil' Will, little brother to the great William Hobbs. It seemed like the entire city knew about my brother; he was a legend and a hero to me and so many others. He was the fastest quarterback at his school and set the record for the most touchdowns and complete passes in a season. Mr. Decker used to tell me "lightning don't strike twice, you can't live forever off your brother's name" and by the end of my freshman year I showed them I was going to be my own legend.

I made it my business to make them all respect me and my name. I studied my brother, but for him it was natural God giving, he didn't work for it. Will just stepped on the field and magic happened, I was good, but I didn't have that. I learned by watching him; I studied his weaknesses just as hard as I studied his strengths. It's easy to teach me the things that made him good, but I also learned from watching him that one wrong quick move can be my last.

The difference between Will and I, was that I wasn't just strong, Will was like a damn freight train, there was no moving him on the field. But me, I was fast; I gave a show when I touched the field, from the time I picked up a football I had one mission; to go pro. I knew my parents worked their ass off just to keep a roof over our heads, they couldn't afford to send me, my brother and sisters to college. I knew if I was going to make it out of St. Louis I was going to need to do it through football.

My sister Olivia married her highschool sweetheart and moved out when she turned nineteen. By the time I started high school the only kids still at home were Ash and me. Ash was pregnant right out of highschool and attended a community college, and my brother was in his junior year at MSU. He was a hometown hero, they always mentioned his name on the sports segment of the local news, the girls talked about him all the time, even our pastor would offer up a special prayer for him on game days. My brother was the man.

He was even there the first time I had sex. That summer I turned Fourteen was a game changer in my life. This chick named Toya really wanted to hook up with Will, but he wasn't really into her. We went to her house, Will told her "my little brother can't go to high school a virgin" and before I knew it she took me in the basement, pulled my dick out and started playing with it. She pushed me down on the couch, climbed on top of me and a few seconds later I had found a feeling I would spend the rest of my life chasing.

When I came back upstairs, Will was watching TV while Toya's older sister Rachelle was on her knees in front of him. She knew we were in the room; she didn't even stop, he just nodded his head at me and I went and sat on the porch. We never talked about that night, to me it was the most amazing shit, but to Will it was another Tuesday.

Will was just a cool ass big brother, who didn't do a single thing wrong, at least he was until he broke his ankle. Not even in the game, he broke his ankle out drunk one night trying to impress a girl at a party. *Fucking tragic.*

He told everyone football just wasn't for him anymore and school was all too stressful, but the truth was my brother knew how to fuck up a good thing. Always have. When he was in highschool, my dad insisted Will help him out at work. "A man that don't work, don't eat". My dad's business damn near ran itself, all Will had to do was handle the scheduling. He couldn't even do that right. Asked my dad to hire one of his boys, who ended up using the building to throw parties and hook up with girls after work hours. Almost ruined dad's good name and all he worked for.

Once he moved back home, he wasn't the same. The corner boys wasn't fucking with him like they used too, the streets wasn't praising him anymore and the only Hobbs talked about was me. He would come to my games drunk and critique my every play. He began smoking weed and drinking more, using our name to fuck the girls at my school and living off of his "I almost went pro" stories. I wouldn't trip, I couldn't. I owed so much to my brother, when I didn't have it or couldn't figure it out, he was always there doing the work for me, but the man he is turning into was a little embarrassing.

I recognized that life had to be more embarrassing for him, twenty-one, back home with my parents and nothing to show for his years in college. He couldn't even hold down a job, he was a football head, that's all he knew, he wasn't in school to actually learn and no one ever cared to ask him what he knew. Maybe that was why my parents were hard on me, but they had nothing to worry about, I had no plans on being anything like him anymore.

When I stepped off the field my senior year, I stepped off with my own name. I was Anderson "The Man" Hobbs. A name that I proudly take with me everywhere I go. It was football that taught me to be fearless, it was football that got me into a good college and it was football that was going to put food on my family's table. Sadly, it was football that ended that dream and it was football that almost ruined my life.

My first week at college had been nothing but let down after let down. I expected to step onto campus and show them why I was "The Man", I was going to be the little brother everyone wanted and slowly grow into the mentor big brother everyone needed, right before being drafted to the league. I was going to show the coach that there was a reason that John Dennings, the talent scout for Texas A&M picked me. Instead, I missed every pass, I couldn't throw the ball right to save my life, shit I could barely outrun the fattest fucker on the field. No one on the team talked to me, even the other freshmen kept their distance. I just knew if I had anything still going for me it was the fact that I never missed with the hoes. But shit, even they weren't giving me any rhythm, I was over it and ready to come home and accept my fate just like Will.

I called home only to have my brother answer, in hindsight I'm glad he did, if anyone knew about failure it was his ass.

"Yo, this shit ain't for me." I grumbled.

"What, school or being away from home?" Will asked, laughing.

"School, football. They keep playing me like I'm some fucking lame."

"Straight? What's happening, who fuckin wit'cho?"

"I mean, it's not just one person, it's all of them. I just can't find my rhythm. The team don't really fuck with me, the coach hates everything I do, and these bitches stuck up as fuck." I argued.

"Oh, shit I thought it was something real, that sounds like it's all you."

"What? This why I hate talking to you, where momma at, put her on the phone"

"Why, so she can tell her baby to come home? You want somebody to baby you?" he mocked.

For a minute there was nothing but silence on the phone. Then Will interrupted the best part of our conversation. "Listen little bro, shit is hard. It's hard going from being the big fish here, only to realize there's even bigger fish out there. You gone have to suck that shit up and learn how to swim or fucking drown."

"What type of advice is that, learn how to swim, nigga I'm a shark?" I laughed.

"Dumbass, that's good advice. It's the truth. You can't come crying to momma every time someone knocks you on yo ass. If you want them to respect you then earn it. Stop being weak as fuck on the field, you embarrassing the family name. You either gone play football or you not. Stop trying to be the big man on campus and focus on finding your rhythm. The hoes will come, the respect with come and if you keep fucking up, you gone be right back here in this bunkbed under mine. Don't do the stupid shit I did, hanging out, drinking, not taking the real shit serious and getting sloppy. It's a ton of people dying for a spot on that team, you can be a fool if you want to and lose it or you can show them why you're there."

I listen, a little surprised, considering he couldn't make this college stuff work. I guess I'm glad he answered the phone; he was right. My mom would have told me to come home, my dad would be encouraging and give me some lessons about how things will magically work out if I tried harder, but maybe not as direct as I needed.

I think if I'm being honest with myself I kind of wanted Will to talk me out of it, and tell me to come home. Instead, he told me how things started slow for him and eventually they turned around and he was right. I mean it didn't happen right away; I rode the bench for the first six games until one day the coach threw me in. The week after I scored my first touchdown, I met the woman who would become my wife.

Lyne'e Riggs. Lyne'e is a sarcastic, thick, chocolate doll that is in my intro to economics class. I've seen her in class before, but I don't think I paid her the attention she deserved until today. Somehow we ended up sitting a few seats down from one another so I could see her up close and personal. I tried to impress her with a few jokes in class, everyone thought I was funny, everyone but her. Lyne'e was about 5'4 and all body. If she was any taller, she would be too skinny for me. She was thick as fuck, the type of body that grew up on cornbread and potatoes, but visually, she was stunning. I think I had been brainwashed into thinking that redbones were the way to go, but looking at her, I was wrong. She has the most extraordinarily beautiful eyes I have ever seen. They are peculiarly luminous, wide, expressive and deep. From the first time she used them to shut me down I was spellbound. I watched her for weeks; she used them like weapons. Mainly at me, even still that was the impressive part. One moment she would let them fall on me gracefully and kindly, then the next she would throw them like daggers to let me know how stupid she thought my every word sounded. Either way, whenever she looked at me, I found myself stumbling over my own thoughts. I had been with a lot of girls, but none had me actually wanting to be with them.

Her smile was infectious, always the biggest and brightest in the room, she has plump full lips, like they were drawn on so it's hard not to have a smile like hers with all the right features. I don't think she was even trying to be as seductive as she is, unfortunately for her, she just was. When she spoke, I hung on every word; I learned more just listening to her, than I ever did from books.

When I finally got past her anime looks, she reminded me so much of my mom. She had an opinion, and you were going to hear it, but her delivery was always gentle and feminine. She wasn't like the groupies I'd come to know over the last couple of years. Throwing themselves on me or pretending to be something they weren't. She was just simply being her and to me she was everything.

Things were as my brother said, coming together. I was finally playing like I had something to prove. I was joining the best brotherhood any man could ask for and although I kept a ton of groupies on my dick, my main chick was a beauty who was as smart as she was sexy.

Yup, the cutie who smelled of lilies and sugar spent her free time riding my dick and keeping me out of trouble. She was exactly what I needed; my age, intelligent, patient, compassionate and the best part, once I opened her up, she just wanted to please me. She had the basics, but by the time we graduated I had formed her tight little paradise into my own oasis. It was where I went when shit was too much, or when I was stressed. Actually, it was where I went when I was happy, sad, mad or my other chicks weren't cutting it. Shit, it even helped heal me after I tore my ACL. It was like her pussy had healing powers and when I was depleted, I could find myself inside of her and be reborn. The one thing you learn being a young black man with a chance to go pro, is you get you a good one and you lock that shit down fast. I learned all too quickly that most of these hoes ain't shit. I can't count how many times after a game or if I was just kicking it somewhere one of Lyne'e girls threw me the ass. None of them cared that I had a girl, none of them cared what I asked them to do, they just did it.

I onced fucked a chick on the bus after a loosing game. She didn't care that I had just got off the field, she didn't care that my boys could see, she just wanted to distract me from the loss. And that was the girls on campus, when I came back home for school breaks, the shit was the same. I can't count how many chicks around the way that let me hit, just because. All someone had to say was Hobbs and pro in the same night and someone's daughter was on my dick in some capacity. It's like they were competing to out fuck the last bitch so they can go pro with me. These hoes out here will use you until there is nothing left to use, all so they don't have to do shit in life. Most of them ain't worth two dead flies, they can either fuck, suck or fry some fish, but very few can do all of that and more. I found one in my freshman year, that wasn't ran through and was just as ambitious as I was. I had no plans on losing her to the rumors or the bullshit. Everytime someone tried to come to her with a story, I'd be more outraged than she was. Every time she'd leave I'd tried to act like I didn't care, ten minutes later I'd be at her door.

If I didn't have her with all of her magic and her wisdom, by my side, pushing me when I tore my ACL my junior year I would have been another college dropout. Constantly reliving the old college glory days of when I "used to be the man." She made me study and try harder so that I would have something else to fall back on in case the Pros didn't come knocking at my door. And I couldn't be more thankful for her and her "healing" powers.

Her Side... The Beginning

I graduated top ten of my class with dual degrees in Finance andDa'vereeting. My graduation was bitter sweet, my dad celebrated and praised me and my overachieving spirit. He threw me a small party with fifty of his closest family and friends and those who couldn't make it were sent the most embarrassing pop up card complete with confetti and ribbon. He made such a big deal about my achievement that it made me feel good. Paulette spent her time claiming I was just looking for attention or trying to outdo my sister. She told everyone that would listen how I am trying to follow in my sister's footsteps, and that she really hopes I can make it work with Anderson since I spent my college years shacking up with him. They were both right, I could have settled for one degree, even though I knew I could earn two. But something tells me she would still be giving this same speech to people, so what's the point?

Besides my degrees, I earned an entry-level position at one of Chicago's top financial advisory companies. Unlike my perfect sister, I chose to go to work. I have never envisioned a life of depending on a man to provide me with anything, something my mother never understood. I didn't want to control the purse strings or be the main proprietor of household responsibilities. Somehow finishing school and working were questionable life choices that needed to take a backseat to Toni getting married. I've always felt like I was my mothers biggest mistake and she reminded me how lucky I was to be in her life every time she got the opportunity. Unfortunately making the decision to move back to IL gave her plenty of time to utilize those opportunities.

From as far back as I could remember she treated my sister and I completely differently. I know my mother loves me, I think if I needed it she would really do her best to get it for me, but I know it would come at a price. Toni and I were three years apart and did not share even one indistinguishable physical attribute. Compared to Toni I'm short, standing at a stubby 5'4 and I've been that height since entering the 10th grade. I look more like my dad and his mother than my mother liked. In fact the only features that I share with my mother are her oval-shaped eyes and her bright alluring smile.

Other than that I was all my daddy's child. I inherited my grandma Diane's cornbread fed body and good full spirit; she has always been my moon and stars. She is the type of woman that will give you the clothes off her back, but will read you your last right just as fast. My whole body resembles that woman, we seem to be divided perfectly by our small waist. My top half is strong shoulders, slightly lean muscular arms, corpulent playful breasts and an almost flat stomach. I'm pretty sure if I laid off the baked goods then maybe I could have a resemblance of a six-pack, but if I haven't had one in the last twenty-three years I don't see one in my future. While, on the bottom there was nothing lean in sight. The words "fat ass" growing up in that house were used so much I didn't learn it to be a term of endearment until I got to highschool. Then I learned I had a "juicy" booty! The same booty that got me kicked out of that bougie ass dance academy my mom insisted I attend or was "so big" that she made me wear belts until I was old enough to leave her home, was now a prominent feature in my life.

Toni and Paulette were both naturally thin, my curves were disgusting to them. Yeah, being thick may be a thing now, but in the late 80's early 90's it was not. "These damn fat girl features, you get from your daddy side of the family." Was something I heard more often than I heard anything positive or pleasant from that lady. I remember all of the girls in my school wearing colored jeans and the company really only made the cute colors in small sizes. There was no lycra in every pair of jeans, you either could fit them or you couldn't. That meant we would have to shop around to find my pair because there weren't many size thirties and above in stock. Toni could walk right in and walk out with every color, and if she found her's before I found mine, sometimes I was just shit out of luck. It took me seventeen years to like my body and nineteen years to accept my body for the way it was and not the way my mother claimed it should be.

My dad told me I was beautiful every day, it was some of the only times I ever heard it as a child. "The world couldn't handle two of me, so God made one of us a girl"! He would laugh. When we would go down south to visit, my grandmother Elizabeth, Paulette's mother, treated me like I was a stepchild. She and my aunts would make fun of my thicker hair, chunky body and my darker skin, while Diane, my dad's mother would show me off. That lady had pictures of me in her church, her job, she'd show me her secret recipes that everyone sought after. She simply loved on me, poured love into me, made me feel like I was a person, a child, a part of a family that wanted me around.

I was able to do well, but not as good as Toni. I could walk in church pageants, but never in one Toni was in. If Toni had dance, then I needed to find something else to kill my time, or maybe wait until next season and see how Toni felt about continuing. The worst part is Paulette was always so clever at keeping me in my place, that even if my daddy did notice, he she had an excuse locked and loaded. Those excuses usually sound like "Lyne'e is only asking because she sees Toni doing it."

Looking back at my life now, I know that's why I tried so hard at everything, I've been trying to gain Paulette's and Grandma Lizzy's love for years. I always wanted to gain approval, to make my mom and her family love and see me how they saw Toni, we were from the same family tree, but I was always low hanging fruit, just never good enough. I was cute, but not beautiful. If only I would have known then what I know now, but then again I guess it made me the person I am today. Ironic life lesson I guess.

Now that school is over and I've earned a position at a great financial firm, I was also engaged to marry an amazing man. Somehow my growth and my accomplishments had finally become milestones for my mother to use. The sad part is as much as I despised her for it, I secretly yearned for it. There have been very few times in my life where Paulette was proud of me and showed it, graduating, the new job prospect and engagement all in one year certainly gave her something to brag about.

Paulette would speak about both her amazingly beautiful and intelligent daughters in her social circles. She bragged to her siblings openly about me and my accomplishments. Grandma Lizzy had nice things to say about me, now my dark skin was "chocolate" and smooth. I was no longer "oh her sister" in a conversation, I was finally "my other daughter". One was a beautiful college graduate who was married to a top engineer for Chrysler. They have a beautiful home and take family trips or have recent additions added to their home. While the other graduated from Texas A&M with a Bachelors in Finance and another in Marketing. She worked for one of the wealthiest accounting firms in the country and was engaged to a smart and successful young black man who adores her. I finally had a seat at the table, it only took twenty-three years of hard work and an engagement for my mother to show any pride in me, but better late than never. I guess.

Upon moving back to Illinois, my parents helped us find an apartment in a neighborhood they both approved of, my dad even paid for our first and last month's rent. Paulette initially put up a fight about us living in sin, but my daddy stepped in and jokingly reminded her of how things were for them in the beginning. That's one of the many things that I love about my dad, he has always been the voice of reason when it comes down to Paulette. He didn't just love me; he fought for me, if she was out of hand or really on her high horse, he always came in like my very own knight in shining armor. Even if it was too late and her damage was already done, he still showed up and did what he could to make things right for me. When it came down to Toni and I he did his best to treat us the same, but I could always tell he had my back. That's what I love about Anderson, he's an ass to most people we come across, but he loves me. He's kind to me, he puts me first. I imagine he will be the same way when we have kids of our own. I can see us having game night, or him holding me while I hold our child. Him rubbing my belly and my feet after a long day.

We will both work, hire a nanny like you see in the movies and go to soccer games on the weekend to watch our twins play. I love that he already tells me how beautiful our daughter will be because she looks like me, and how little A.Hobbs is going to act just like him. I love him even more knowing that he knows my ugly, and he still wants to be here with me. I don't think I'm damaged by any means, but I know I have some emotional scars that are visible and he still sees me, the real me and stands beside me.

When we are all together and Paulette is on one, he holds me a little tighter. He made it his business to pay my parents back for the apartment and that made me love him a bit more. Even after my dad insisted he use the money to buy me something nice, Anderson still paid him back, and he did it while taking time to bond with dad at a football game then out to dinner.

As a little girl, my dad always told me to pick a good man, who loves and cherishes me, and I think I did. I found a man who finds any sliver of my skin and gives me the softest kisses on it. A man who holds me in his arms at the perfect times and runs his fingers through the tips of my hair for no reason other than he loves me. I found a man who reads me books with me on rainy days, or who stays just close enough to me that he is able to reach out and touch me at any time he pleases.

I'm certain this is not the type of love my daddy was thinking of when he suggested I find a man who loves me, but I did find a man who loves to make love to me and who can't get enough of me. Living together was nothing like our life on campus. Waking up to him everyday, knowing when I get home, he's there and waiting. Not having to limit our conversations, the amount of time we spend together, or how often we touch one another. There is no one here to make us feel like we're being extra, for once we can make love and be as loud or as rough as we want to. We can take our time and enjoy one another without having to worry about who will be coming home and when. I never knew how much I like being held until we started just sitting on the couch watching tv and him pulling me so close you can't tell where he starts and I stop.

He and I have always hung out together, hit up a club or a party, but it's usually with a group. Now it's just me and him, but somehow we have more fun now than before. I've met a few new girls since coming back, and sometimes I will link up with my girls from highschool, but living here as an adult. That's different. I've come a long way from sneaking clothes out the house or lying about where I'm going.

His Side... The Beginning

After graduation, Lyne'e and I moved to Chicago. I couldn't imagine moving back home after graduation. One great black Hobbs as a failure was enough. I had no intentions of continuing my life in my brother's shadow. Every time I see him, he looks worse and worse. Thankfully I have Lyne'e and she has our futures all mapped out. We shared a small one bed apartment that her parents helped us find and a beat up old Neon that my cousin Brian gave us. I have a few cousins that stay in the area, but we couldn't be any different if we tried. My cousin Brian was cool, we used to be really close when we were kids, but life took us in different directions. Brian was all about being in the streets, when my mom had us in school and every free class she could find, his mom was working extra shifts and he was on the block. Not just him, his dad, my uncle Bernard was the same way. It's cool having someone here and not having to rely solely on The Riggs to help us out, but it always seems to come at a cost. But Brian, he looked out, just to make sure I was cool.

Our Neon was a little red piece of shit, but it got us everywhere we needed to be. The first couple of months we really didn't go anywhere, we spent our time planning ways to take over BDI Investments. BDI is one of the lead financial advisory companies and their headquarters are in Chicago. She and I both applied for entry-level positions, one of her uncles knew a guy and could get us in the door, we had to do the rest. We sat up nights imagining how set our lives would be once we became CEO and CFO of the company in ten years all while raising our two kids in Deerfield with a summer house in St. Lucia.

I couldn't imagine my life with anyone else, honestly she is damn near perfect. Her smile, those eyes, her short little legs, and that fat ass. Most days it's hard to keep my hands off of her. She's always soft, her skin feels like buttery velvet and she always smells amazing. Rather she's walking around in one of my shirts or her sexy barely there panties, Lyne'e is always the most amazingly natural beauty in the room. She comes from a good home, she's educated, can cook and there is nothing she wouldn't do for me plus my momma loves her. Every time I watch her in her own little world I get more and more excited for our future. I can't wait to see her carrying my child, or watch her playing with my curly head bright eyed daughter who will look just like her. Most of these females out here my age be on the same thing, gimme, gimme, gimme. I hear my boys talk about what they had to buy a chick, or giving some girl money for hair or nails and it makes me appreciate Lyne'e even more. Not only does she wake up breathtakingly beautiful, she doesn't not need a bunch of extras to look good. Bare toffee tone face with her hair in a bun she's easily outdoing most of these hoes I see everyday. Plus she is independent as hell and has been from the jump.

Shit, it's been times I've had to ask her for a few dollars in school, and she had my back. My boys were spending every dollar they had to try to get a girl, meanwhile mine was holding her own. The moment we moved into our apartment, she devised a plan for us, we worked harder than planned and saved every penny we could. We wanted a big wedding and she even agreed to wait a few years for it, and if I could get her to wait a little longer, we would have a nice size down payment on our first home a month before the wedding.

Neither of us started out making much, we walked out of college making the bare minimum. What we did earn was enough to get by, pay the rent and that was good enough. Half of our income was used to pay the bills and our day-to-day expenses; we divided the other half between the wedding, our savings and down payment for a house. We had a plan, a goal, a life that we both wanted and we knew working hard was the only way to get it. Our sacrifice wasn't just financial, we worked like dogs to come up in the company as well.

Butler D. Irwin was the CEO and still the top investor for BDI. Upon first glance Mr. Irwin was intimidating as hell by any stretch of the word. There was almost never a time that he was alone or a space where unwelcome guests like myself were welcomed. From the weekly videos he sent to boost morale and keep us "in the know" he has thick silver hair, permanent wrinkles in his forehead as if he spent his life disapproving of everything, tiny blue eyes, thin, tightly pierced lips and a prominent chin. Every once in a while I'd catch him smiling at something and forget for a second that he was the man in charge around here. It doesn't happen often, he has a very childlike smile, he looks like he was a ladies' man when he was my age. His shirts are always a crisp white and the top two buttons always undone. He spoke with his hands, but he does not do a lot of talking. He keeps a team around him that knows how to take orders, and for some reason they all wear a lot of black.

We were hired together but worked in different areas of the company. Lyne'e found herself in the financial analyst department. It was actually the best move for her and it gave us some time apart. I on the other hand had been lucky enough to be placed in one of his smaller teams in the financial risk department. It was a few steps under the area Lyne'e was in, but it happened to be an area that Irwin frequented. He liked to be ahead of the curve and he felt the best way to do that was to be aware of any risk that may be coming down the pipeline. Most of the newcomers on the team were used to run errands, prep for meetings that they were not allowed to be a part of or to take notes. I knew I would never get a moment of his time running errands and greeting clients, I needed to stand out. We needed to stand out. We were both young and black trying to jump ahead in a white collar and white company with no experience, if either of us were going to move ahead, we would have to do something outrageous.

Sunday's are our busiest days. Church in the morning, laundry at her parents in the afternoon, home in time for dinner and the game at night, usually followed by her for dessert before we go to bed. This particular Sunday we ordered in and I watched the game while she polished her toes on the couch. After the game she flipped through channels with her feet in my lap and I scrolled through my phone waiting for her to make a move. She stopped on CNN just long enough for me to see a familiar name. Seattle Moore Mutual. I knew a little about the company because I'd written a paper on them for a finance class. The paper was about the company going public and the incredible Christmas bonuses they gave their employees, but now according to the news report they were in financial trouble.

It took a few weeks worth of calls and emails, but I was able to secure a meeting with the chief operating officer of Seattle Moore Mutual. Lyne'e and I took a personal day and flew to Seattle to meet with Sean Miller to discuss a different approach on how we or maybe an angel investor like BDI could help the company not only stay afloat, but become marketable again. I don't know what made him take time to meet with us, but I was beyond thankful.

Having Lyne'e there couldn't do anything but help. The way she analyzed numbers on the spot was impressive, but her real talent was marketing. I never understood why that wasn't her real passion. She could easily count cards and use her powers for evil, but that's not who she is. By the end of the day she showed Miller where they were losing the most of their money, compared a few of their public and private books and was able to come up with some ways to save the company money and possibly keep most of their employees. She spent the entire flight going over their numbers and recalculating new ones.

She explained how she could even reach out to some old school mates and brothers from my fraternity to help find some new investors. Mr. Miller loved what we had to show him and agreed to get back to us in a week or so after talking things over with his team. All we needed to do was get Irwin on board.

I spent weeks purposely bumping into Irwin's assistant Johnathan around the building. He was a scrawny little pale face guy with frosted tips and pointy shoulders, who I'm pretty sure in his downtime is in a boy band cover group. I let him talk my ear off about his favorite rap artist and Emma Lathan, the pretty brunette that he doesn't stand a chance with over a few beers and could find out Irwin's schedule for the week. I casually ran into him at his favorite restaurant while carrying my BDI backpack and complimentary baseball cap and introduced myself. Irwin fell right into my trap and invited me to sit down where I proceeded to tell him about my findings and my interest in Seattle Moore Mutual.

I explained the benefit of investing in a company like SMM and explained how lucrative the investment could be. He was particularly interested in how the public would view him for saving hundreds of jobs. I made sure to touch on all of Irwin's points of vanities, including his incredibly full head of silver hair. When we both were back in the building, I presented him with my findings and waited for him to review them and get back to me.

The next two weeks were torture, constantly waiting for a call, hoping that when he see's me he'd want to talk. Pumping Johnathan for any information I could, but it was clear he was now using me just as much as I was using him.

Shit had been a little off between Lyne'e and I, she didn't love how I didn't include her in my pitch to Irwin, but she understood it was a now or never thing. I explained that I just happened to run into him and I needed to jump on the chance to speak with him. I knew she didn't love it, but Lyne'e was all about the bigger picture. Eventually she came around, but I'm sure it was only because she wanted to fuck. Lyne'e didn't stay mad for long, my sweet little innocent girl was now a full on freak. Even if she wanted to be mad, she couldn't go a full two weeks without sex.

We got up early one morning to get to the gym at BDI before the crowd rushed in. We haven't had sex in days, and the amount of tension between us is unbearable. The best thing for the both of us is the gym. Besides I love working out with her, Lyne'e is a competitor by nature, she'll do her best to keep up with me, but she never could. The upside is when it's all over, she's covered in sweat and can't keep her hands off me. Unfortunately the gym filled up before I could get her out of her sticky shorts.

Later that afternoon I got a call upstairs to Irwin's private suite. The building we worked in was beautifully crafted and very modern, but Irwin's suite was magnificent. It occupied two floors pulled together with floating winding stairs and hardwood floors that shined like mirrors under the top chandelier and steel gray walls. Floor to ceiling windows, a fireplace and a fucking baby grand piano. How much money do you have to make to place a baby grand piano in your office space? My mouth dropped the moment I saw it. I couldn't imagine what had to happen in order for someone to play it, but I wanted nothing more than to be the reason it was played.

"So tell me Anderson, what is it you want out of your time at BDI?" Irwin asked as he waved me into his office.

"I want this, I want all of this, I want an office in this suite and to leave my name on something great." I replied with a smile surely big enough to show all of my teeth. The fact of the matter was I wanted to be Irwin, I wanted all of his pretty assistants running to get my dry cleaning and coffee, I wanted powerful men standing around hoping that I looked their way, I wanted to be so important that I could have a fucking baby grand piano in the middle of my office for no damn reason.

I watched as Irwin pulled two whisky glasses from behind a desk on a shelf "I think you have potential, my team and I have gone over your numbers and looked into Seattle Moore Mutual and to be honest, you are right. The media would love the fact that we have saved hundreds of jobs and added to our financial advisors in addition to taking over millions in loans, it's a complete win for all involved. Quite frankly I'm impressed that a newcomer fresh out of college could not only see the bigger picture, but had the initiative to put together such a splendid plan and to present it to me so professionally."

"Thank you, sir!" I replied as masculine as I could.

"We are going to get you moved up to Bullock's team, you will report to him and you will make sure he has all the information and help he needs." He advised while pouring me a glass of his specially aged whisky. "The upside is this move comes with a raise and a promotion, consider yourself the first entry-level employee to move this fast in our company. I am impressed."

"Again thank you sir!" I replied as we both toasted to my success. It was happening, just as planned.

I couldn't wait to tell Lyne'e what happened. On our ride home, I was like a kid on Christmas morning. I was super excited as I explained how Irwin loved my ideals, recanting his lame ass jokes that I had to laugh at and how when it was over, he shared his special whiskey as we toast to my success. I was on a wave. You couldn't tell me shit, I can't remember the last time I saw all thirty-two of my teeth let alone showed them like I was doing today. I spent the entire ride home talking, so much that I didn't notice Lyne'e uncharacteristic silence. I turned my head to see her gazing out the window as if I hadn't said a word.

I watched for a reaction as I threw a couple of lies about how much I could make, thinking if nothing else would get her attention the money would, she said nothing. Instead, she checked her nails in the sunlight and picked at them intensely over replying to me. You would think she'd be happy, this is what we worked hard for, instead she's sitting here ignoring me like I'm some bum ass clown pressing her for her number at the gas station. I wanted to ride this high just a little longer, but I was so fucking irritated by how she's acting I turned up the radio to my rap shit she hates to hear after work and rode home quietly fuming.

When we walked in the apartment nothing had changed, this was the longest I had ever known her ass to be quiet other than in her sleep, and even then her snoring ass made more noises than she's doing now. She took her time hanging up her coat and placing her things down as if I wasn't even standing there.

"I'm gonna take a shower and go lay down, I'm sure you can manage to fix yourself dinner." She said with a half ass smile and a low tone.

I didn't even answer, and she didn't wait for me to respond either. She sauntered out of the room as if she didn't have a care in the world, turned the speaker on in the bathroom where she stayed for the next hour. Every minute brought me closer to actual fire coming out of my ears. I walked a groove into the floor trying to think about what I could have said or done to get us here. If college didn't teach me anything else it taught me to keep my shit tight, so I knew there was no hoe's calling and telling her anything real. These past couple of months I've been so busy working I haven't really had time to kick it with my boys that much, so I haven't been in the streets. It wasn't a holiday or anniversary that I may have forgotten. There was no reason for her ass to be acting like I just fucked her sister.

When she got out of the shower she walked in the kitchen humming a song and two stepping, ignoring my venomous stare not even two feet away from her. She tightened her towel around her chest before bending over to grab a slice of cheesecake she had hidden in the back of the fridge. I fought my natural urge to knock that shit on the floor as she reached around me to grab a fork out of the dish rack.

"Are you serious?" I snapped. "What the hell is wrong with you?"

She said nothing, turned on her heels and headed out of the kitchen. I lost it. "Lyne'e what the fuck, so now you don't hear me talking to you?"

"Anderson, do us a favor and lower your voice, I can hear you and when I feel like talking to you, I will. Why don't you go find something to do with yourself other than fuck with me." She warned.

I watched in shock as she walked down the hall. "Are you fucking crazy, seriously if there is something wrong with you mentally you need to let me know, now."

"Oh now I'm crazy? I've known you for years and now I'm crazy? Well, why don't you leave my crazy ass alone." She replied softly before closing the door.

I couldn't figure out what part was making me more angry, how calm she was or how she's handling whatever is pissing her off. I stormed into the room and turned the TV off from the box. "Why don't you just say whatever is bothering you, you were perfectly normal until I told you about my meeting with Irwin, what the fuck, you jealous?"

"Jealous?" She asked, throwing her cheesecake and plate. "Jealous of what, some shit you couldn't get without me and then turned yo black ass around and sold the ideal as if it was yours."

Oh, that's why she's mad. "Lyne'e I didn't sell it as my ideal."

"Really, so Irwin thinks we did this? Is that why he's promoting you? Why you and him were sharing lame ass jokes and drinks? Because he thinks we did this? You're a fucking lie. Is that why you never mentioned to me that you were going to speak with him about our ideals and research? Why yo black ass knew for weeks that this was happening and you never said a fucking word to me?"

I wanted to reply, but I had nothing. I actually tried to remember if her name even came up.

"That's what the fuck I thought. You went in for yourself, you've been looking out for your fucking self this entire time. I've been working my ass off to help us grow and the entire time you were using me. That's how you treat me? Me, Anderson?" She yelled, tears flowing from her eyes. "You a selfish ass muthafucka, and I've always known it but I never thought you would do me like that." She wiped her eyes before telling me to get out and leave her alone.

The next morning she was gone before I woke up. I saw her in the office and she said nothing to me, in fact she looked at me as if she didn't even know me. Sure she is angry with me, but she has to see the bigger picture, we are a team and if I get a promotion; it benefits us both.

Within the next few months news was circulating about BDI and Seattle More Mutual. How just before the holiday season, hundreds of people will be able to keep food on their tables due to BDI investments. I used Lyne'e calculations to justify keeping so many people employed and although I tried to explain that she assisted with the calculations Irwin and Bullock just did not seem to care at this point. I sent flowers to her at work and left the card blank, but she knew they were from me and left them at the front desk. We lived together but apart, the more I grew in the office the further I failed in my relationship.

I hadn't made my way to the executive suite or procured an office just yet but Irwin made me lead on a few more projects and even agreed to make Lyne'e head assistant on them as well. I thought that it would have helped clear the air between the two of us, maybe help get me some, but she was hell bent on not fucking with me in any capacity. Every step I took seemed to have knocked us back three steps, the only thing that saved us was the fact that we both were working super hard on our projects so we didn't really have time for one another.

Her Side… The Exploring

I would be lying to myself if I said I wasn't more than pissed at how things turned out with the Seattle Moore Mutual project. I did just as much work, if not more researching and gathering information. I alone ran and compared all the numbers, compared yearly fees and expenditures, and prepared reports showing the benefit of taking on the failing company. Yet Anderson was the only one who benefited from my work. I found the investors, small or not, I found the extra money that was needed to keep costs down and for that I got nothing. The last year has been nothing but stressful and infuriating. Anderson spent most of his time on the merger and under Irwin, when we get to speak it's usually to argue about something that he feels he's too busy or good for. To make matters worse, Irwin keep putting me on stupid ass assignments, causing me to waste my degree preparing spreadsheets and grouping sample loans for an upcoming audit or worst to sit and patiently wait doing fucking nothing in meetings. Hell, I'm black and a woman, maybe it helps him reach his minority quota or something.

The worst assignments are the ones that made me an assistant to Anderson. I can't determine what pissed me off more, being an assistant to Anderson, a C student at best assistant or the fact that I couldn't get out of it. He knew I wanted nothing to do with him, so he used those opportunities to "try and fix it" as he continuously mentioned or pointed out. But the part that really gets me, that really lets me know it is time to leave, is him using these times to put me in positions that I had to listen to him. I can't call him any inappropriate and demeaning names while at work, I had to force a pageant smile, when I really wanted to blow his shit out.

His new life changed our entire way of living. Suddenly he needed new work clothes, because he was "growing" in the company. "I can't keep showing up wearing the same basic khaki or black pants, I need to make a statement." When the wardrobe changed for work, the shoes needed to change too. Of course alone with our strict budget he couldn't afford the clothes he wanted, so he had to dip a little into one of our Holy Trinity accounts. Money he always claimed he'll put back but never does. When I ask him about it, he just blows me off and claims he is making enough to cover it, but whatever money he's making rarely makes an appearance in our home or bank accounts.

As if that wasn't bad enough, his new way of life doesn't leave any time or interest in me or any other plans, like our wedding. Most days I only see Anderson on the way to work and on our way home. And if it's a weekend, he's out with Da'vere and this new circle of friends. Thankfully Paulette dreamed of nothing more than throwing an extravagant over the top wedding. Usually her and my taste were nothing alike, she's ostentatious where I was more clean and classy. It works in my favor that she sees me as "boring and simple" as she often described my fashion over the years and went with a more subtle approach. These days Paulette was acting more like a mother than I was ever used to. I was able to confide in her, laugh with her and actually seek her opinion in counsel, not just about the wedding but my new life with Anderson. Even though things with her and my dad were the worst I have ever remember seeing them, she was still very family oriented and wanted Toni and I married to loving men.

"But, I really don't think that I can get over what he's done, I feel like he stole from me." I whispered into the phone trying to keep my business down and not floating through the halls of BDI.

"Sweetie, he saw a window open and went through it. Yes it was wrong, but you don't throw away your future based on one mistake. He did wrong, he acknowledged it and he apologized for it, let it go." Her words seemed to twist the knife that Anderson left in my back further and deeper. I don't know why I expected any different, my mother has always sided with anyone over me and if that anyone was of the male persuasion I was left stinking. "If he wants to do the heavy lifting, let him. Let him work the long hours, let him drive himself crazy in that rat race of a job, meanwhile you spend that money as fast as he can make it. Since money means more to him than being a good partner and showing you some loyalty, then hit him where it hurts. If you still feel betrayed."

I pulled the phone from my ear to make sure I was speaking to the right person. These are words Paulette Riggs would never utter. "Lyne'e? Lyne'e? Can you hear me?"

"Yes, mother I can hear you, just a little surprised it's you saying any of this."

"Well, don't be, if you start letting him walk all over you now, he'll be doing it forever. Put your money up, find a savings or a good investment, put as much of your income aside for a rainy day and you use his money for everything else. And the day he parts his lips to say absolutely anything about money, light into his ass. Remind him how he got where he is and who he fucked over to get there, and in a few months, maybe years, you are your daddy's child, you will have moved on and forgot all about this. But you do not throw away a good man over a mistake, you're just making it easy for some whore I didn't raise to come in and reap all of your hard work."

This Paulette I recognize, she was vengeful, spiteful and petty. More importantly, she was right. I could spend the rest of my life bitter and angry at Anderson or I could accept what I can't change and move forward. If he wants to do all the heavy lifting, who am I to stop him? I can think of a million things that I would rather do with my money than paying bills and now I will.

Playing the lead assistant in the Anderson Hobbs show left me a ton of free time. At first I thought it was going to be hard, but after I noticed how unbothered he is with our time apart, it made it easier for me to careless. During the day I'd work, during the evenings I'd hit an after hour with a few work friends and still make it home in time to prepare a quick dinner. Our days used to be planned down to the very last good night, but now he's in bed hours after me, and most mornings catching a ride with someone else to work.

So when I couldn't have another drink, eat another appetizer or tell one more guy I was engaged, I spent my free time planning our wedding. I needed something to keep me preoccupied. Work wasn't really a challenge, so it was either throw myself in the planning or throw myself out a window. For the most part, I made all the decisions in our lives, he just showed up, wrote a check and carried the bags. It gave him something to brag about with his lame ass friends on their lame ass guys' nights. He is finally becoming the man he's always wanted to be, his bank account is growing, he is the new "it" guy at the job, and although he thinks I don't notice, the girls around the office are following him around. He's happy and too busy to cheat, I suppose I can adjust to our new reality.

My mom got us an interview at a venue that I absolutely loved, but they only allowed walkthroughs on Thursday afternoons or day of events so that people could get a feel for the place all done up. I worked a lunch into our schedules about two weeks ago to assure he didn't pull some last-minute crap like he had been doing with most things these days. Paulette picked me up because Anderson was already out meeting with a client, so he agreed to meet us there. I was in love from the first sight; the sun shining beautifully displaying lush shades of greens from the perfectly manicured trees and lawn. The flowers laid out flawlessly creating a natural aisle leading to a beautiful altar created with asymmetrical flower arrangements and draping for an airy backdrop. All of which pale in comparison to the absolutely beautiful waters of Lake Michigan dancing ever so seductively in the distance. I hadn't even stepped inside of the venue and I was already imagining every moment of our future and out "I Do's". The space was in the perfect location, it was not too far downtown Chicago, but still in the area with ample space to park. But the best part was the space was within our budget. We both agreed that we'd rather have a large house over wedding debt, and Paulette knew someone who knew someone that agreed to give us a hefty discount.

By the time Anderson showed up we were done with our tour and the coordinator was handing me the venue's brochure. He stepped out of the car on the phone and he walked over to us the same way. I wanted nothing more than to be angry, but that was all my mother needed to see me fighting with my betrothed publicly. As if it wasn't bad enough he was late beyond belief, he had the nerve to step to the side and finish up his conversation before making his way over to us. He smiled brightly at the coordinator while tucking his phone inside of his suit jacket and reaching her hand out to shake her hand. She was a very attractive older middle eastern woman, who appeared just as irritated by his lack of effort as I was. Everything about her was calm and subtle, but you knew she had money. Her two-carat diamond cushion earrings and Channel loafers were very delicate accents to her Dior sunglasses and matching handbag.

"Sorry I'm late, I couldn't get away." I knew that tone, that was his bullshit to come tone. He leaned in to kiss my mom on the cheek and whispered how beautiful she looked in the sun. It was obvious by the look in his eyes I was about to be swimming in Anderson bullshit for the rest of the day. "Baby can we please get together and talk about this later tonight, I really need to get back to the office." He asked, taking the brochure from my hand.

"Wait, what? No, do you know how long I've been waiting to get into this place?" I asked, following behind him as he pulled his phone from his jacket pocket.

"I know, and trust me I feel bad, but I really need to take care of something." He pleaded not even looking at me for real. "When we get home tonight, I'll look over the brochure while you tell me all about this place. It looks pricey, but Paulette seems thrilled so that's a plus."

It all happened so fast he didn't even give me a moment to reply. Apparently he drove miles out of his way to tell me he can't stay for the appointment that we made weeks ago. I spent the ride back to the office fuming. There was really no reason for him to show up, let alone to cancel our plans. Now I have to ride back to work while Paulette lectures me on how to be a better wife and how I can be more accommodating like Toni in her marriage.

"I mean your sister is always having to adjust to meet Avory halfway, but that is what a good partner does. It's not easy, it's a thankless job, but once you become a wife and a mother you will realize not everything is about you."

"Ma, what are you talking about? Toni is two steps above a simple servant and all you do is complain about how daddy doesn't consider you. Do you really think that is the type of life I want?"

"Your sister has a very successful husband, who gives her anything she wants, including a car so that her mother doesn't have to drive her around." She barked.

For the rest of the ride I didn't say a word. What was the point? My first mistake was thinking she and I had turned a page, followed by me inviting her along and last but not least was not cursing Anderson's black ass out on the spot. Had he not ditched me, I wouldn't have had to even ride back with her. I couldn't get out of her car fast enough.

When I walked back to my desk, I couldn't help but notice Anderson was not at his. His keys and jacket weren't even there, which means he still hadn't returned. There was no way that I could have beaten him back if he actually came back to the office.

Since he never showed up at the building, I ended up catching a ride home with Ebony, a girl who stayed near us. Later that night, he came home, took a shower and went to bed as if nothing happened. Not a single word about blowing me off nor anything about why he was clearly taking a half day and never told me. I was so angry I couldn't sleep, at least not next to him without planning how I could murder him and get away with it. I slept in the living room for the 1st time and he didn't even notice.

The next morning we rushed around the apartment not saying anything to one another. If he walks into a room, I hurry and walk out. It was as if someone had removed the wool from my eyes, there was something going on in my relationship that I must have been blind to until this very moment.

Once he had me stuck in the car, he pulled a typical Anderson move.

"Listen, I want to talk to you about the wedding."

I felt my stomach starting to slowly descend as I turned to look at him.

"I think it would make sense to push the wedding out another year. I know it's not what we planned, but I think it would be good for us." He continued, while bruising his hair in the mirror.

"Are you fucking kidding me right now? You can't be serious." I snapped.

"Yeah I am, waiting another year would allow us to make a larger down payment on a house, have the wedding that you want and as a bonus an island for our honeymoon."

"Anderson, where is this coming from? I never asked for a big wedding or an island honeymoon." I'm pretty sure I could have made sense of what he had to say under different circumstances, but something about this whole thing right now, just set fire to my soul.

The part that really pissed me off was his delivery, he never even looked in my direction when saying it. He just kept bobbing his head to the music like he was in some fucking nineties R&B music video. I regained awareness for a moment in time to hear the end of his speech. "I just want to have time to invest in us and you, how I should. Working long days and even weekends now to prove to these folks that I'm the right man for the job. Shit, baby you know when they see me all they see is a young black boy,, not someone worth a seat at their table. I'm the least likely candidate for these jobs and I have to work harder than the rest, baby you know that?" He continued while brushing his waves in the mirror again. "But when we do it, you know our shit gone be fly as hell."

I was devastated, shit I was fucking furious. I've only been this complacent because it was what we needed for the moment, now I'm supposed to sit around and wait for him to get back to me? The rest of the way to work I didn't say a word, I couldn't get my thoughts together to even form the words, and he was so self-involved as usual he didn't even notice. He pulled into the parking structure humming along to the stupid song on the radio completely oblivious to the hurt on my face or the tears in my eyes.

We walked into the building together and separated as he walked towards his coworkers. I think he mumbled bye, but couldn't be sure because his back was to me as he walked in their direction. This was becoming more and more common. At work he behaved as if I didn't exist and at home he barely made an appearance. The only time he was home and really present is when he's trying to fuck and even that wasn't what it used to be. I'm twenty-five, stuck in a lackluster relationship with a man I loved, but for the first time wondering if he loved me back. Shit wondering if this is actually love or just the motions. I know the tale, if you want anything good you have to fight and sacrifice, blah, blah, blah, but I feel like I'm the only one with a sacrifice here.

Aside from Shalynn, most of my coworkers were all older women, married, or have kids and can't get out. My best friend was miles away, taking over a law firm and conquering mountains and I have found myself in the role of the boring basic bitch in The Anderson Hobbs show. My life had turned to boring shit. At twenty-five.

I met Shalynn at work; she was super cool and chill. We couldn't hang out much because she was also in school full time and a mom, but she was fun. We'd meet up for lunch or walk down the street to the coffee shop where she would catch me up on the office gossip that I often missed. Anderson couldn't stand her, he never really had a reason, but still he didn't care for her. The feeling was mutual. She wasn't disrespectful towards him, but it was clear she could take him or leave him. Moreso leave him. Over the past year she was one of the few people that I could really talk to about anything. She worked in a different area of the firm so our paths didn't cross professionally, but she completely understood the politics.

She grew up in Chicago so she knew all the best places to eat and hang out. She and I were both the same age, and had a lot of boyfriend drama. Hanging out was an escape for the both of us. Shalynn was the youngest girl of five, her boyfriend was cool from what I could tell but had absolutely no drive or passion for anything. He wanted to be in the streets and wanted her at home. He had a legit job and made some money, but nothing compared to her. Her relationship issues are different from mine, but sometimes the tunnel looks clear when you're not in it. Plus, it was nice to have someone to talk to who could remotely relate.

For the past couple of months most of Anderson's "great" ideas came from me. My ideals for old accounts, my take on how we were marketing our brand, shit I even recall hearing him share my stories as if they were his. I remembered my dad telling me there is a fine line between a valid complaint and unreasonable whining. Anderson was making me feel like I was whining, on our rides home I found myself yelling about everything and every time he made it seem like I was being paranoid or childish. The day he claimed I was jealous, was the day I finally met my breaking point. I can't complain or argue not another day. It was more clear to me today than at any other point in this relationship that Anderson will never see me.

"Ms. Riggs, Anderson asked if you could order lunch for the team from that Asian place he likes?"

"Excuse me"? I replied to the girl now standing in front me.

"Anderson said to please order lunch for the team from the Asian place he likes. He said you have his card and to put the lunch on it."

I watched as this woman proceeded to speak to me as if I was an idiot. The same woman who walks around hanging on Anderson's every word. The same woman who is in every meeting, at every lunch, who is always a little too close.

"No I understand English, what I don't understand is why am I ordering lunch for your team. Isn't that something you should take care of?" I asked, trying not to let my mouth say what my face and brain was thinking.

"Well, we're really busy and I thought you could take care of it." She huffed.

"Hmmmm well, the time that you wasted coming to find me, could have been used to order lunch for your team." I snapped before picking up my desk phone to call Anderson.

"Anderson speaking." He answered.

"One moment." I paused. "Is there anything else?" I asked Kelsy.

"I'm waiting to give you the orders."

"Kelsy, please walk away from my desk. I do not work for you or Anderson. If you want to order lunch, I suggest you go do it somewhere else." I forced a smile, before returning to my call. "Now let me get this straight, did you really just send Princess Malibu Barbie to my desk to ask me to order lunch for you and your team?"

"I didn't think it would be a big deal. Are you busy?"

"You've been doing a lot of not thinking lately. You don't have a credit card Anderson, who do you think was going to pay for this lunch for you and the team you work on?"

"Lyne'e fine. I'll take care of it." He snapped before hanging up the phone.

Not only was I one of a few black women in the company, but I'm one of the youngest. In the past eighteen months I have watched my fiancé grow like a weed in this company most of which for my ideals and hard work. To make matters worst, I'm constantly treated like a fucking secretary in the 50s. The shit was degrading. There was almost never time to show any potential I had because they always assigned me to bullshit jobs. And I know it's at the request of Anderson's black ass. Anyone who knew me, knew me as Anderson Hobbs' girlfriend, not even his fiance. Management was so scared of a nepotism or a sexual harassment suit they didn't promote me. Now this mothafukka has me ordering lunch for him and a group of people off my credit card.

I didn't hear from him for the rest of the workday. I waited at the front door for him like I always do for about twenty minutes before Kelsy showed up to tell me he needed me to catch a ride home with Shayla or Ebony. At 5 o'clock people go running from this building like it was on fire, and she knew that. I can't tell which one of them did it on purpose, but waiting until twenty minutes later was intentional.

WHEN I WALKED THROUGH the door at our apartment, I was furious. I looked around for Anderson, but of course he wasn't home yet. I called his phone only for it to go to voicemail. I was so angry I could feel the blood under my skin burning. It was more clear today than ever, I can't stay in this relationship like this. This was beyond disrespect, he was now letting his people treat me like I wasn't shit and that was not cool.

When Anderson came home, I had gone to bed and locked the bedroom door. The next morning he was sitting on the couch waiting for me to come into the living room.

"Good morning to you too Lyne'e."

I didn't respond. I continued to the bathroom and locked that door too.

"Are you going to tell me what I did this time?"

"What you did? You're not serious I know?" I hissed. "Anderson, you left me stranded at work. You didn't answer when I called you, three fucking times. And then you walked in this fucking apartment at eleven thirty." I yelled, opening the door to look him in his eyes as he lied his way out of this one.

"I'm a grown ass man, I didn't know I had a curfew." He barked. The tone in his voice let me know he was prepared for this fight. This wasn't self defense, this was premeditated. You only come to a fight prepared, when you know its going to happen.

"Fuck you." I said pushing past him. "Fuck you and your fucking curfew. I didn't know if you were dead or alive somewhere and your response to me is that bullshit." Even replaying the millions of random thoughts I had last night brought tears to my eyes and I hate them. I know he's going to view them completely differently than their intent. I didn't even have time to be hurt, because I was too fucking worried. Last night. Today, knowing that his muthafucking ass is alive, I'm angry. That means he knew what he was doing.

"You're right, that wasn't called for." He tried to apologize. "I went to get us something, and it took longer than I expected."

I ignored him and continued to get dressed.

"So you're going to ignore me. I'm trying to talk to you."

"And I'm done talking to you. You don't have an ounce of fucking respect for me, I get that now. You had a chance to talk to me yesterday after you sent your bitch to tell me to order y'all lunch with my fucking money."

"Your money, don't we both pay the fucking credit card bill?"

"Anderson move." I demanded as I walked to the door. I pulled my phone out and called Ebony as I walked down the hall.

The entire day Anderson and I crossed paths, but I'd instantly turn and go a different way. At the end of the day, Anderson was waiting for me at the front door. We typically try not to bring our home shit to the building, but today I was ready to risk this job and my freedom to fight him. The more time I had to think about everything the more angry I became. Looking at his self-righteous face the more I wanted to slap him in it.

"I sent Ebony home, so you have to ride with me." He laughed.

I said nothing. I took a deep breath and began walking towards the garage.

"No, we are over here." He pointed with his arm.

I looked around for our little red shooter, but didn't see it. What I saw is him pointing at a brand new 2008 Black Benz. "Anderson what is this?" I questioned.

"You like it? I thought it was time we upgraded. I'm so tired of meeting clients in the Shitter or having to call a car service. The shit was embarrassing." He smiled boastfully as he held the car door open for me.

"Anderson, we don't have money for anything else, we put the wedding on hold, but you can go buy a new car. You don't even think to talk to me." I did everything I could to hold in my anger.

"I did this for us, we can't go another Chicago winter with that car and you know it. Plus, you keep making it seem like I need your permission for everything. Yesterday at work with 'your' credit card, I didn't come home the time you thought I should. And now this. Damn Lyne'e, what can I do right?"

I wanted to take his argument seriously until I remembered him telling me that the ring I wanted would be too much right now to finance. That pissed me off, but not nearly as pissed as I was when I looked over at him and realized he was too busy posing for the car next to us to really be as mad as he seemed. The best thing I could have done was to ride home as quietly as possible.

I made dinner like I would have any other night, I also made a plan. I've worked so hard to get out of my sister's shadow, out of my parent's house, out from under Paulette's controlling thumb and now I'm still not my own person. It's clear there is no room for me at BDI investment so I secretly applied at Burnett and Weinstein, one of the top accounting law firms in the country. I expected to be waiting for weeks for a reply, but it only took a few days. By the next week I got a call from their HR rep about the position I applied for. Shaylynn let me borrow her car to get to the interview because every time I so much as mentioned driving Anderson's he had a reason not to let me. My breaking point had bent, broken and crumbled some more, I needed out of something. The idea that paying for this car will come from our joint account or our joint future and I couldn't touch the damn thing made my inner city girl try to creep out. But I'm sure if I bust the windows out, I'll just end up paying for the replacements. One thing I learned from my parents is that wars aren't won off instinct and emotions, they're planned.

The morning I received my welcome email we drove to work together as it was another day. I listened as Anderson rambled on about how Bullock was an idiot and couldn't do his job without him. Ironic right? And I gazed out the window gleefully planning my escape from BDI and laughing to myself as I imagined Anderson trying to shine without my ideals to help him glow.

I didn't even give him a chance to say bye; I skirted off to the elevators and made my way upstairs to human resources. I secretly gave my two-week notice and asked that my leaving be handled with respect and discretion. I'm pretty sure Michelle, my HR rep, thought I was being beaten at home, and I was about to make a run for it, but I couldn't care less. All I wanted was to get through the day and on to my dinner plans that night. By the end of the day, the only people who knew about my new plans were myself, HR and Shalynn. Even HR hugged and congratulated me on my future endeavors, all that was left now was to get home and tell Anderson.

I was so excited, I could feel actual weight being removed from my chest. I couldn't wait to tell him of my plans. After work Shalynn gave me a ride home, she came in for a quick congratulatory glass of wine as I began preparing a special dinner complete with a bottle of wine that I didn't buy from the corner store and candles.

"I can't believe you're leaving me in that place alone. And with Needy Nicole at that. If I don't have you to walk with, her ass gone think we're best friends and try to hang out with me." She laughed walking her wine over to the couch.

"You act like I will not be two blocks over. So what I'm hearing is if we don't work together you ain't gone be my friend?"

"Shit, you act like once you make all that money, you gone have time for me." She replied. "Plus Anderson ain't gone let you hang out with me anymore."

"Shut up!" I laughed. "Anderson, don't run shit, especially me. You can always come with me once you pass the bar."

For a moment we lived in silence, I guess thinking about what our new lives would look like.

"Well, call me tomorrow and tell me all about tonight. I'm about to take this buzz home, see if I can't find someone to give some too!."

She hugged me tightly before disappearing down the hall. By the time Anderson came home she was gone, but I was either too buzzed or too happy to care. I fixed our plates while he put his things down and sat at the table.

"You know I had that mee...."

"Hey, for once why don't you start with *Hi, or hey babe, how was your day?*" I instantly interrupted him, slamming his plate down in front of him.

"My bad, did you have a bad day or something?"

"No actually, I had a great one, so great I decided to do all of this." I said motioning my hands around the room "but as usual, you can't go a moment without talking about yourself long enough to notice".

Anderson's forehead wrinkled as his eyebrows formed double lines and he pressed his lips tightly together before he took a long deep breath. "Sorry Lyne'e, I had a long day. I really don't want to fight with you. How was your day? What happened that was so magical?"

At that moment all the air in my balloon had gone, along with my appetite. He was so fucking condescending and disrespectful that I couldn't take it. I don't think me asking him to focus his conversation on me was too much. I felt a lump rising in my throat which only meant soon tears would start to fill up in my eyes making this moment even more disappointing. "You know what, never mind. Enjoy your dinner!" I sneered as I dumped my plate in the trash and walked out of the kitchen. I could hear him yelling something, but I was too busy trying not to cry as I grabbed the car keys off the hook and stormed out of the apartment.

He called me at least a dozen times, but I knew the calls weren't about me as much as they were about the car. I drove around in circles, so angry all I could do was cry. It wasn't that moment; it was all the moments. How did we go from two college kids in love, to whatever this is today? Before I knew it, I was at my parent's house, but I couldn't pull myself out of the car to go inside. Something told me my mother would treat my good news with the same interest that Anderson did and I was not in the mood. Plus, I really don't feel like hearing how pathetic I am because I supported myself over supporting Anderson. Hell if she hears me at all, with Toni pregnant with what I am sure is being treated as the second coming she probably won't even hear me. Feeling alone was not new for me, but something about this feeling was. I threw the car in drive and pulled off as quietly as I pulled up.

I took one call and as usual she couldn't have shown up at a better time.

"Bitch!" Sloane yelled through the phone.

"Oh my God I miss you, where are you?" I asked, wiping my tears.

"My plane just landed, I'm getting my bags and about to go grab me a cab."

"Aahhhhhh" I screamed. "No, you're not, I'm on my way to pick you up now."

I turned the car around and headed to O'Hare airport. I don't know how in one of the busiest airports, the first person I see is my dear best friend. I pulled into the half of spot in front of her; I didn't even care that the car was sticking out in the middle of the street and I didn't even care that I almost didn't put the car in park. I hopped out, keys in the ignition and ran into my friends' arms. We hugged so tight I thought one of us would pop. I didn't care who saw us, or what else was going on in the world, I was so happy to have one person in my life who loved me.

We put her things in the trunk and pulled off before the airport security could make their way to us.

"So what are you doing here?"

"You first, what's wrong?"

"Nothing its fine, we'll talk about later. Now talk woman."

"I'm moving here. My uncle's firm need fresh blood and I can't stand being away from you. So here I am." She said, smiling and throwing her hands in the air.

"Oh my God. Girl. So are you staying with me?"

"You know I can't be under the same roof with Anderson. Besides, I have a place. You know how my dad is, he had to approve first. So while I finished up things back home, he found me a spot in Hyde Park."

"And you just moved, sight unseen? You're not even concerned?"

"About what? My uncle has already picked out the basics and had things set up. You know I don't travel without my gun. I'm good."

All I could do was laugh. This woman is the only person I know who is this fearless about everything.

"Plus, we both know the moment I call Da'vere he is going to come running. If he even thinks I'm going to let him close enough to see an imprint, he'd build me a city. Horney little toad."

"Ugh I can't believe you let him touch you." I shivered.

"Well, what can I say, I was bored one night, he was there and needs were met. If you find something to put in his mouth, he's not that bad. Plus that man hung. Like it makes no sense."

"Yuck Sloane, come on, I don't want to know this."

"Shit, you should. I can't figure out why someone like him had to be blessed with the biggest joy stick I've even seen. Only problem is he has no real clue what to do with it. You have to throw him on his back and do what you can with it. If not, you'll be in for a night of fumbling around, grabbing things that aren't meant to be grabbed. A bunch of twisting and turning. Ugh or mindless humping. He fuck like he's in a porn."

I watched Sloane's silly ass as she imitated some of his moves and we laughed all the way to her new home.

The next morning I woke up to Anderson sitting at the foot of our bed watching me sleep. The sun lit the room brighter than any of our lamps ever could. Anderson's eyes always seem to dance in natural light. I wanted to lay there and pretend to be asleep just a little longer, maybe to avoid this conversation that was sure to lead to a fight, but I really had to pee. I crawled out of bed and pushed past him as if he wasn't there.

"Lyne'e what is going on with you? It's like nothing I do is right." he asked while standing at the bathroom door.

"Anderson, can you honestly tell me the last time you asked me about my day?" I questioned flushing the toilet. "What about the last time you even pretended to be interested in what I have going on? The only time you have any interest in me or my thoughts is when you need a fresh new ideal to spin in Irwin or Bullock's face?"

"What the fuck, this shit again?" He interjected.

"Yes, this shit again, you used me to come up at work, played me like you were doing it for us. You fucking ignore me like I'm some random ass bitch following you around and when we're at home, you spend the time talking about you. What the fuck is right."

"I didn't use you, we worked on Seattle together..." he retorted while running his hands over his head.

"Yeah, together and then what did you do?" I asked, washing my hands and turning to look him in his face as he answered. He stuttered for a moment and then said nothing.

"You see that? You have nothing. You can't even explain that shit to yourself. Anderson, you didn't get over on some random person, you got over on me. I yelled trying not to cry, well trying not to ugly cry because the tears were coming out rather I liked it or not. "You fucked me over. And you did it so effortlessly. Even if Irwin did not know who I was, it was your job to make him know me. To tell him you didn't do this alone, to let him know you didn't come up with any of this shit on your own."

"But..."

"But nothing and I accepted it, I closed my mouth and played my part. Then what did you do, you canceled our fucking wedding. Without even talking to me, even asking me. You made a decision that affects us, but we never agreed to it."

"Lyen'e the fucking wedding is not cancelled. We have moved it to another year. Come back here." He yelled following from room to room behind me.

"Tell me one thing about our wedding, Anderson. Tell me the colors, tell me the place, can you tell me how I feel or shit how I reacted to you showing up ninety minutes late to our meeting and telling me you want to push it back another year." I searched his face for an answer, for any form of feeling, there was nothing. "Now you're speechless, funny. Yo black ass ain't ever fucking speechless when it's time to talk about you."

"Lyne'e I'm sorry, you're right. I have been taking you for granted at work and at home. It's just been work, I wanted so badly to make this life for us I didn't realize how I was treating you. I promise, it won't happen again." His entire face softened, his eyes widened and his words came out clear and true, for the first time I believed him. He placed his large hands around my waist and pulled me in close to him. "I swear, I'm truly sorry."

"I believe you, but only because yesterday was my last day at BDI, I start my new position at Burnett and Weinstein next Monday." I interrupted as I broke his embrace. Anderson's eyes rolled over my face like wheels on freshly dried cement. I kept waiting for him to ask a question, yell, curse or anything, but he did nothing. He cut his eye at me while pulling his statuesque frame away from mine and slowly stomped down the hall.

I couldn't determine if I had successfully gotten the response that I wanted or if I had bit off more than I could chew, but either way I had laid the gauntlet and a fight was soon to follow. The apartment was quiet, cold and thick. I could feel actual chill bumps forming along my arms, I didn't fear him raising his hand to me. Anderson was a man, not an animal, though I felt something coming. I went to the kitchen to make a cup of tea; I glanced at the clock on the microwave now needing to call Michelle and tell her I'm not even going to take the two weeks. I was simply done. When Anderson turned the corner. I stood as tall as my legs would allow and pushed down the growing ball of anxious energy in my stomach. If I was going to be ready to defend my honor, I would need to be level-headed when I do.

Mt. Hobbs blew. "Why?" he asked, grabbing a banana off the counter. I recognized the expression on his face, it was one that I had often seen on my mothers, disappointment. And just like that I was taken back to my childhood and trying to please Paulette. It's always been about pleasing someone else, I had done nothing wrong, I took initiative in my own life and did what was best for me. Something that I clearly will always have to do, protect and do for me.

I placed my mug down on the counter next to the stove and dropped in my favorite tea bags and without even looking into those big brown eyes of his replied "Anderson, you are sorry now, over a year later. But you aren't sorry for how you treated me, you're sorry for how I feel at this moment. If we had to do the entire last eighteen months over you wouldn't do anything different, but maybe spend a little more time with me. You went out and got what you wanted, you fucked me over to get it and now you are on your way to the career you want. I wish you well in that career, but I will no longer aid or help you in it another day. I don't even understand why the person who supposedly loves and cares for me would want me to continue to fail while he succeeds. What I can't understand is why the fuck are you coming at me as if I have done something wrong by doing the same?" I asked, pouring the water into my mug. "Really what is the difference? I didn't fuck you over to get this new position? You wanted me to sit around and watch you shine? Do you really think I came this far to be a hoe on your sideline, have I ever? So yes, while you were running in behind Bullock or Irwin's ass, I was negotiating higher pay, more vacation time and yes an office." I paused. "And do you know why they agreed, because I'm worth it. Because I have something to bring to the table and they see something in me. I'm using my own natural talent to propel me for once, why is that a bad thing?"

He looked me directly in the eye after everything I said and nodded his head while saying "Yup." That's all the energy he gave what I had to say. Yup. I should have taken that "yup" and walked away, but I couldn't. "Anderson I did not do all of that studying and working in college just to sit on your sideline and if you don't understand that or can't respect it, then clearly you and I have bigger issues."

"You know what Lyne'e, since you're so bitter that I am growing and you're not, then I wish you the best of fucking luck."

A WEEK HAD GONE BY without us saying two words to each other. This wasn't the man I knew, he was cold; he was distant; he was unresponsive. That week turned into a month, we slept in the same bed, but there was nothing between us but space. He was different; we were different. He took his phone with him everywhere he went; he began coming home late and sleeping on the couch. A month had gone by and he hadn't even so much as rolled over hard and touched me by mistake. It was then that I knew it was over, even if he came home every night physically, emotionally he was never there. I told myself that I would never give my all in a relationship while someone else gave nothing. I watched my dad live that way my entire life, and it was horrible and lonely. It was not a feeling that I was willing to endure.

I wanted to win the war and the battle, but there was nothing here to win. He and I were the stars and the moon, I wish I could have said fuck it. I would have given anything to have him hug me, to show me he cared and was proud of me, but I got nothing.

I packed my things and was gone when he came home from work. I left the little ring he gave me in college on his nightstand and his keys on the counter.

His Side... The Identifying

I knew I had let things go too far between us. Especially after Da'vere told me he saw her having coffee with some guy. Time may heal old wounds but it can kill the vibes and lines of communication if allowed. I should have been happy for Lyne'e when she got the job at Burnett and Weinstein, but there was something in me that just could not get past this feeling of betrayal. Maybe I should have expressed to Mr. Irwin that we both worked those accounts instead of taking credit, but it was easier to play the game in the boy's club than to reinvent the wheel. She should have seen it that way. There was no need for me to be aggravated and uninterested whenever she brought up the wedding. I could have watched one of her dumb wedding shows with her like she asked. I guess I could have put more effort into the little things, spent more time with her, been more pleasant to be around, made a big deal about her accomplishments and the holidays. Shit looking at it, I could have done more.

Admittedly, there were a lot of things that I could have done differently, but that's easier said now. It's funny how you see things more clearly in the storm than you do when everything is sunny and shit. But I guess it's too late for all the things I should have and could have done, she clearly has moved on.

I made a promise to her and to myself that I would be the type of man my father was; I watched my dad work his ass off to give us everything we needed. As a kid I had my entire future all mapped out, I knew I wanted a family and a career. I wanted to be the type of man that people looked up to. I've invested entirely too much time, effort and energy into the two of us to walk away now. These hoes I keep running into are all for show, pretty faces, fat asses but don't have shit I need. I could add them all together and they still wouldn't be my equal. In the past year I have put ten thousand in my savings, bought my first new car, and earned two promotions at work. I can walk into any bank and walk out with whatever I want. At twenty-five and I have a better credit score than both my parents and most folks twice my age. I've worked too hard to just bring someone new in for the ride.

I tried to brush off what Da'vere had to tell me; it sounded more like him hatin than him being useful. He's always had bad vibes when it came down to Lyne'e and I. He never said anything bad about her directly to me, but I saw the way he looked when she came around, I noticed how he changed when we were all together or when I spoke about her. I don't think he was jealous of me for having her; I think he hated the way she pulled me away from him and my boys. He was all too eager to tell me about their run in at breakfast.

Lyne'e is simple, she really doesn't ask for much. She just wanted the family life that she didn't have growing up. Her fucked up ass momma ain't nothing like my mine. Plus, I know Lyne'e would love our kids like my mom did us, all she wanted was a family and security. Simple things her dad provided, simple things my dad provided, shit any man worth anything should be able to provide. And here my dumbass go and fuck that up. I was never supposed to let her get away from me.

I'm not surprised she was able to negotiate all that she did with her new company, Lyne'e is the shit. She's always been headstrong and super smart, she could have easily out earned me at BDI if given the chance. Subconsciously maybe that's why I always kept her at bay professionally, I was worried she'd outgrow me. Thinking about it, why the hell didn't I see that as the plus it is? I don't want to spend the next thirty years carrying some grown ass woman who can't do shit but get on her knees or make reservations. Besides, Irwin is all about that family image. They all are, offices filled with family photos and memorabilia, but if you're in the office early or late enough, you get to see who's fucking who. I'll never be able to make these men trust me if I can't show them I'm one of them. Alone I'm a threat, I look irresponsible, but add a wife to the mix, especially one as smart and beautiful as Lyne'e and I look like I'm ready to lead the free world. I'll never make it to a top office here or truly find myself in Irwin's good graces if I can't show him I possess some basic principles.

This apartment is quiet, too quiet. It doesn't even smell the same. Plus, if she's dating it won't be long before some fuck head try to make my girl, his. I need to get my baby back, besides I'm going crazy in this apartment alone. I miss our quiet nights; her reading something smutty, with her legs in my lap. Or me playing the game with my head resting comfortably on her ass or in between her legs. I've literately had the pleasure of fucking her against every wall in this apartment, now I can't stand the sight of them without her here. Every time I bring some chick back here, I find her making herself a little too comfortable in the spaces that belong to Lyne'e. When I got home from work last week, I saw Chantel parked outside. I can't have Lyne'e coming back here to crazy psycho thriller bitches parked outside our home. I pulled my phone out and scrolled through my emails looking for an old message Lyne'e sent me. I remember she was super excited about a house she saw, but I was either too busy to ever go look at it, or just didn't think I was ready to settle down for real, for real. *Got it!* I searched the address and found the realtor handling the sale.

To: Sonali Shama

From: Anderson Hobbs

Date: 05/18/2010 10:09 AM

Subject: Available listings

Hello, I am interested in the property listed on Western Pl in Highland Park, Il. If the property is still available please contact me, could you please get back to me? If not, and you have anything else in that area, you have my information, I would love to view them.

A. Hobbs

To: Anderson Hobbs

From: Sonali Shama

Date: 05/18/2010 1:17 PM

Subject: Re: Available listings

Hello, Mr. Hobbs the property on Western has actually sold, but I have another property around the corner that you may love. If you have time today, I would love to show you the listing. Below is my contact information, please call me set up a time.

Sonali Shama

Shama Realty Co.

(555) 825-8914

THE HOUSE WAS PERFECT. I met with Sonali after work and she showed me a beautiful three story brick house with a two-car garage, five bedrooms, four baths and a kitchen big enough to satisfy the pickiest cook. The house was a steal at three hundred thousand, thanks to a bitter ex-wife looking for a quick sale. I knew once Lyne'e saw the place she would love it too. The neighborhood was well manicured and family oriented. There were children playing outside on their bikes, nice cars parked in the driveways and neighbors waving hello to one another. It was nothing like where we grew up. No oil stains in the driveways, no shoes hanging from the wires, no police sirens or helicopters circling above. There were no couples fighting on the front porch while their kid played dangerously close to the street. I didn't hear bass thumping from the cars and more importantly there was not one abandoned building or house in the area. The neighborhood was the perfect place to slit my wrist due to boredom and for a nice nosy neighbor to find my body just in time to still be casket sharp.

From the time I pulled on the block I felt like I had entered the twilight zone. It was the kind of neighborhood I had always heard about but had actually never seen. I knew it was the type of place Lyne'e would love as well. She grew up in a pretty decent area like this one, their house wasn't half this size, but the neighbors were all welcoming and interacted with one another just like this one. Plus, I'm sure her boogie ass mom would love this place, all Paulette cares about is an image and keeping up with one. She wouldn't care if I beat Lyne'e and moved in my side bitch as long as I did it in a house like this one with a smile on my face and money in my bank account. Besides, Toni and her new husband just bought some crazy big and expensive house and it's nothing like this one. Their house is cool, but it's old, dated and according to Lyne'e and her bitter ass momma, is walking distance from his parents.

It was the perfect place for me and my family to live; I had worked hard to get myself out of the hood and this home proved exactly that. I could see us hosting dinner parties for clients and our babies taking their first steps here. This house will be perfect in the first step into the new Anderson Hobbs.

Sonalli told me what the current offer was, and I offered five thousand higher, there was no need to show me any more properties and considering the low asking price, I'd rather not wait around for anyone else to snatch it up. On some level I know deep down I was dead ass wrong for the way things had played out between Lyne'e and I. She didn't deserve the things had done, and if I was going to show her I had changed, I needed to show her more of the life she wanted.

BDI offers special financing plans to its higher ups, and I was on my way to being one of those. My first meeting of the day was with Irwin to discuss a new project he wanted me to supervise. I casually let the Open House flier slip out of one of my folders as we left his office. I know he likes to discuss new projects on Mondays at his favorite bar for lunch and if I wanted to get in his good graces, this would be the best time to do it. After the bill came and all the other kiss-ass's were pretending to need to go to the bathroom, I showed him some interior pictures of the house. He did all the things I needed, raved about the area, told me about him and his wife's first house and last but not least told me to call Mrs. Amy Phiper in loan processing. He continued to explain that she will work with me and take care of anything I need so as not to distract me from my new project.

The following day Amy and I met for lunch to exchange information. She was nothing like I expected, Irwin seems to keep a certain type of woman around him, artificially beautiful, tall, thin, long hair and fake tits. Amy was not even one of those things, she wasn't even nice; she took my information, paid for her coffee and walked away.

THE CLOSING PROCESS was pretty cut and dry as well. Ms. Sakks was all too willing to sell her ex-husband property. Her bitter ass made things all too clear for me. There was no way I was putting Lyne'e name on the deed. And although I will give her anything she wanted, we are definitely getting a prenup. Not only did this Sakks lady sell the house drastically below the market value just to be spiteful, but she gave away all of his shit too. She was nice enough to leave the place damn near furnished. She gave me the warranties for the new kitchen suite, washer, dryer and the contact information for the companies who had recently remodeled the joint.

"We just added a fresh addition to the back, created a mother-in-law suite, installed an intercom system throughout the entire house and had the pool resurfaced." Ms. Sakks grinned.

"Ms. Sakks."

"No, please call me Becca." She interrupted.

"Sorry Becca, that is a lot of work to have completed on a house only to sale it at this rate, is there something I should know about the area?" I asked, accepting the bottle of water she held out for me.

"No, sweetie the neighborhood is wonderful. We've been here for six years and my husband grew up here. It is his family's house." She mumbled while rolling her eyes.

"Which again, makes me wonder why you're selling it to me for so little? Don't get me wrong, I love it, and I know my fiance will die when she sees it, I just want to make sure know one will come knocking at our door soon." I pointed out.

I watched as she laughed and walked slowly over the cabinet bypassing the bottle of water that she had just opened. It's clear she is a well polished beautiful woman, clearly young but far from naïve. Without hesitation she pulled out two wine glasses and placed them on the granite countertop. She took a few steps to the wine cooler that I didn't even notice behind the island and pulled out a very expensive bottle of wine.

She never asked if I wanted a glass, she simply poured us both a full glass of wine and placed mine in my hand. "My dear husband told me he couldn't have children and didn't want any. We never spent time with his family and he had no interest in mine. My husband moved me hundreds of miles away from my family so that he could be closer to his, and I came with no hesitation. He wanted a housewife, I became a housewife, he wanted to be more sexually free, I allowed him to disrespect and degrade me. I agreed with him when he asked for one with my friend. He claimed that monogamy wasn't for him or a healthy way to live so I accepted. He swore our lives could really be perfect if my friend agreed to be with us more. Despite my every nerve telling me "no, run" I asked, and she agreed. She lived too far away, so he insisted she come stay here with us, again every fiber in my body said run, it's not worth it. Instead, I stayed." I watched as she wiped tears from her eyes before gulping down her glass of Pinot. "He needed her and I to be even closer, claimed that he could feel the tension or resistance in me, told me I was being a prude and bringing down his morale, so he paid for trips for the three of us. Checked us into hotel suits, the three of us and one king size bed, he ignored all the strange looks from people because they were just *jealous*. As if it wasn't bad enough that he had tricked me into this relationship with my closest friend, he managed to make me the third wheel. The addition to the house was because we needed space. The Mother-in-law suite was built because leasing an apartment was a waste of money and Carrie needed a space that was her own. To his family Carrie was my friend that I needed around because I was lonely, so his mother saw me as childish and insisted that I needed to grow up. I needed to be a wife and stop trying to hang out with my friends. Meanwhile, she saw Carrie as a delight and seemed to make her son laugh. This beautiful nightmare went on for almost two years, when it was over I didn't even recognize the woman I had become. I went home to Montanna to help my mom with my dad after a heart attack and came home to find my dear husband with my friend standing in the kitchen rubbing her pregnant belly. The man who didn't want children was beaming with so much pride over his bundle of joy that he didn't even pretend to stop when he saw me standing there."

For a moment we stood there quiet, me staring at her and her staring at a space by the refrigerator. I don't know what I could say that would ease the tension in the room, but I understand why the steal on the house a little better.

"I called my daddy, who was an attorney himself and I walked away with everything. I still had every text message asking, begging and bartering my morals for his filth. I still have the diamond watch he had engraved after convincing me to got rid of our child. *Time changes, we won't.* A fucking declaration of the life he wanted from me. Carl didn't even put up a fight. Suddenly he's a family man, who's so elated to be a dad he didn't want any drama around him and his pregnant fiance. Can you believe it, he and I were still married, and he has a pregnant fiance. They all tried to fight to keep the house, but the house was a gift to him, and I was added to the deed as security and a thank you for getting an abortion right after we married. Because he claimed a kid will just slow us down." She laughed. "I don't even want the fucking house, but I refuse to let him or his evil mom have it. That's why I wanted a quick quick sale, I don't even want to bother moving any of the things out, you can have it all. Do with it what you want."

She gave me a big tearful smile and the keys before walking out the house with her glass of wine in her hand. I walked around the house taking it all in; the place was pretty bare, there were a few rooms that had some left over items, but nothing that I couldn't dumb on trash day. I remember Sonali telling me about the husband cheating, along with the appraiser and even Amy cracking a smile as she spread the gossip, but I don't think I heard the story with so much detail until today.

I thought she was bitter before, today I think she might be nuts. It wasn't enough that she divorced him; she had to tear his reputation down too. Sad, just move on, you got the house and clearly a shit ton of his money. All for some shit she was into, when the dust settled she was out and her girl was in, *fucking bitter.* I can't count how many times I had suggested to Lyne'e that we have a threesome and not one time did she go for it. You can't trick a woman into eating a pussy or sucking a random dick, that's some shit she wants to do. I think the problem was her girl was better at the shit and dude figured out where he really wanted to be. Did he deserve to lose his house and half his money, no? Could he have just divorced her before she gathered a mountain of evidence on him or before he knocked up his side piece, yes. Lose everything he and his family worked hard for, naw, that's just too far.

I took a couple of days off of work, called up a couple of my boys and moved our things, or what was left of our things into the new house. Although Ms. Sakks was cool enough to leave it furnished. I didn't want any of that shit. Especially after knowing they was having orgies and fucking all over the place. My boy Craig took the furniture, Da'vere found some artwork he liked, some golf clubs and workout equipment in the basement. Once everything was stripped, we painted the walls white to give Lyne'e a blank canvas. I want to save the decorating for her; I know she loves doing that type of stuff. She had me watching every do-it-yourself or home improvement show that came on tv when we first moved into our apartment. The only decorating I did to the house was in the adjoining room to the master bed. I bought a baby crib and painted the room a soft gray and a baby yellow just the way Lyne'e once described our baby nursery to me. I remembered she hated the ideal of a blue or pink room from the stories she told me about her childhood home. If nothing else I've done shows her I'm ready to do things between me and her right, this nursery should. I even remembered the stuffed baby elephant she wanted in the corner. *She's going to love this shit!*

Her Side... The longing

I had a plan, well we had a plan, but nowhere in that plan did I imagine I'd be looking for a place on my own. Sloane couldn't have moved her at a better time if I'd planned it myself. There was no way I was moving back home, I can hear Paulette now "your sister is living in a mansion with her perfect husband and you're here on my couch."

Ideally I would find a place like Sloane's, private, out of the city and gated. I love the city, but one thing I know for sure, this is not the place you want to be coming and going late at night alone. I'm sure I can't afford this neighborhood, but I make enough to find me a cute small place of my own. Once I took my share from our joint account, I had a pretty decent amount. I could easily put a down payment on a nice place, but I really don't know if I'm ready to buy a house just yet. Plus Sloane insists I go through my "grieving" period here with her.

It's been hard. I can't lie, I try to fill my time with as many distractions as possible, but at night the loneliness kicks in and I find myself in my feelings again. Sloane is alone, and she's happy that way, I love that about her. She is the face of independence. Keyla likes to pretend that she's happy single, but she throws herself in and out of relationships so often that I just don't believe it anymore. She is full on head over heels, bussin' it wide open, tattoo his name so they know it's real over a guy one day and the next she's over it. I think she wants something but has no clue what it is, and I love her for it, but that's not me either. The only person who I deal with that I can relate to is Shaylynn. But lately her and her dude have been in a good space and I don't want to disrupt that with my shit.

The truth is, I hate sleeping alone. I'm used to Anderson's warm body next to mine. I've been using his heart beat as white noise for so long that I don't know how to sleep without it. The smell of his pillow is something I never imagine that I'd miss. Him pulling me close to him and throwing his leg in between mine so that we are connected. I miss us. And there are no words that I can use to explain any of this to my friends to get them to understand, because they don't get it.

The up side to staying here with Sloane is I don't have to completely be alone. Plus, this girl signs us up for every fucking self-defense, workout, dance it off class she finds. In the past three months, I've finally managed to lose my little pooch and tone up a bit. At least if I do ever get out there and start dating again my body will be snatched.

Plus work has been pretty good too, making the move to Burnett and Weistien was the best decision I've ever made. The work is easy; the people are relaxed and I've even earned my first promotion which came with an office and the assistant that they promised me. There's some balance in my universe even if my love life ain't shit, professionally I'm killing it.

"So, what's going on with the guy, is he here?" Keyla asked as we stepped off the elevators.

"Yeah, but I think they went for lunch."

"I'm so proud of you, this place is nice." She smiled as she walked around my small and underdressed new office. "Get some pictures or something in here, break it in, you've earned it."

"I know, but most of my pictures are of me and Anderson." I barely got his name out of my mouth before she rolled her eyes.

"Well lucky for you, we have that trip to Miami coming up. Cause yo ass need it. How long are you going to keep moping around? You refuse to talk to the hot guy here, you turn down more niggas than a bank offering credit and that's when we can get you out of the office. It's time to move on." Keyla demanded as she walked back over to my desk. "I get it, trust me I do. You and Anderson had something. That shit was clear, but you left for a reason, it's time to let it go." Keyla advised with a warm smile and a gracious caress of my hand. I know everything she is saying is coming from a good place. She doesn't really like Anderson, but she has always tried to give him a fair shake.

I walked Keyla back downstairs and out the building before heading to my next meeting. She is a paralegal for a firm a few blocks over so we get together for lunch once a week. One my way back upstairs I ran into Jamal Wells and a few members of his company. I had been avoiding him since they arrived earlier this week; he asked me out the last time he was in town, but I was too into my feelings still. The man is fine as hell; he has that street nigga turned corporate vibe and I love it. You can tell that he smokes weed, but not too much, because I know his job does random drug test, he's smart as hell, and from what I've learned one of the youngest and only black men at his company. That don't say shit for diversity on their behalf, but it does mean he's not a dumbass. We all stood waiting for the elevator together, I indulged in small talk with his team as he stood quietly in the back of the group. Every time my eyes made contact with his I could feel the butterflies in my stomach making a run for it. This man made me feel like a little bitty girl. I'm sure I was blushing, trying to focus on every word Randle from his team had to say. But there he was when I looked away again, his eyes fixated on mine, as if he could see right through the unbothered mask I had put on. I offered an innocent smile, hoping that would be enough to get him to look away so that I could breathe again, but the salacious smile he offered back made the butterflies fly further south than I expected. Once on our floor, I excused myself to the restroom to clean up the moist mess left by Jamal's smile and the sneaky butterflies. As I washed my hands, I took a hard look in the mirror, ran my fingers through what is left of my curls before telling my inner self to pull it together.

I spent the rest of my day trying to avoid any direct contact with Jamal. It was bad enough that I was horney as hell and hadn't had sex in months, and good sex even longer, but there is nothing I hate more than wet panties. I was one more long stare away from taking them off and stuffing them in my pocket; I don't think I could take anymore of him today.

"Knock Knock."

I looked up from my desk to see who could be asking me to do something this late in the day only to see Jamal standing there in his black sweater and slacks. As I waved him in I noticed he kept a chain tucked in his undershirt and that both his ears are pierced but he only wears a diamond in one. I love that it's not so big that he looks like an idiot walking around looking like an idiot and not too small that he looks ridiculous. Clearly he has a style that he leaves outside of the building and that style was clear by the leather jacket that he had in hand. I don't think I've seen him come or go from the building so I never noticed his coat.

"Come in." I said as I pushed some papers to the side and tried to catch my eyes from wandering even lower than where they were. "What's up, did you need something?"

"Yeah, this isn't a work stop, I just wanted to stop in and say hi. I feel like we've been missing each other all day."

I paused before blurting out something crazy. He didn't need to know that I was avoiding him, more importantly he didn't need to know why. "Yeah, it's been a day around here. One fire after another, I haven't really had time to focus on one thing. I'm sorry about that."

"No problem. How about you let me take you to dinner?" He asked, while slowly sitting back in his seat. For a brief moment I imagined sitting on his lap but snapped out of it long enough to hear a reply come from my mouth that even I didn't expect.

"Sure. That sounds nice"

"Bet, Um, let me run and get rid of my team and I'll meet you out front around five."

Again, words flying from my lips as if someone else had taken over. "Yeah, how about you meet me at my place, that way I can get out of these clothes?"

"Oh, so you're finally letting me take you on an actual date, huh?" He smiled. "Well in that case, how about I pick you up around seven?"

I knew the smile on my face had to be the most embarrassing smile I'd ever given. I'm pretty sure I'm showing all of my teeth, but I couldn't control it. Shit, I couldn't control it or my body. Instead of responding like an adult, I just nodded my head and watched as he walked out of my office.

As soon as I pulled out of the parking structure I called Keyla, but of course she was busy. Her boss is such an ass and has a bad habit of assigning her stupid ass assignments at the end of the day. I quickly hung up and called Sloane.

"Girl."

"Oh this should be good, what happened?" She whispered.

"Ugh are you still at work? I need to talk."

"I am, is it bad?"

"No, I'm about to go out with Jamal, the guy from work, and I'm freaking the fuck out. I don't know the last time I went on a date with someone who's not Anderson." I yelled in a genuine panic.

"Well first, don't mention his name. Second, you've got this. It's a meal with another person, who happens to be sexy as hell. So don't wear shit from your closet." She laughed.

"Shut the fuck up, I hate you!" I laughed.

"Girl, ain't nobody trying to fuck Mother Pearl from the Youth Center." She continued to laugh as she gasped for air.

"I don't know why I called you."

"Because, you know I'm not lying. Now go to my closet, find you something to make you feel sexy that Anderson has not had his crummy little fingers on already. Fix you a drink, take a warm shower and do your makeup. Relax. You're beautiful, he knows it already that's why he's been sniffing around for weeks. Call me before y'all leave, and make sure Mike at the gate get his plate and license."

"Relax." I repeated a few times out loud.

"Yes Relax. It's just a meal."

I went home and did everything on Sloane's list. Made me a drink, took a shower. I tried on the black lace panties Keyla forced me to buy and made my way down the hall to Sloane's closet. If this girl don't do shit else she shops. Her closet was the stuff of dreams, everything organized by theme and then by color. She had a little black dress for every occasion. I tried on a few and settled with a black sweater dress and a pair of chunky boots.

By the time Jamal was at the door I was two tequila sun rises in and more relaxed than I needed to be. The moment I opened the door and saw he smiled at me I felt tingles flow throughout my body and settle in an unused space of my body that I didn't even know was there. He reached out to grab my hand and the moment I felt his skin touch mine I could feel my thighs weaken and what felt like water flowing from my core. I've felt nothing like this from something so simple as a smile and such a simple touch.

"You look beautiful as always." He whispered as he leaned in to kiss me on my cheek. The closer he was I could smell soap and his cologne. I see the chain that he wore under his shirt now outside and resting nicely around his neck.

I took a deep breath of him while he was still closed before asking him for a moment to freshen up before we left. I darted up the stairs to my bedroom to change panties again, this time something less sexy. Maybe these will be the reminder I need to keep them on throughout the night.

"Sorry, I'm ready." I advised as I ran back down the stairs.

We spent the night laughing and listening to one another's back stories. We've talked a bit here and there previously, he knew I was getting out of something; I knew he was dating. Tonight we dove deeper into those conversations. It felt good to talk to someone who not only knew how to talk back, but was willing to listen. I didn't have to lead the conversation and when I wasn't talking, he was actually engaging in conversations about real shit. So many times Anderson and I would be out and he wouldn't have anything to say, but would accuse me of not talking to him. Or he would monopolize the entire conversation and pull out his phone when I was speaking. For the first time in a long time I was having a real adult conversation with a man who was actively listening to what I had to say.

We ended up closing the restaurant down. We sat and talked for hours, ordered random things on the menu just to try them and then we'd talk some more. On the drive home it occurred to me that this night had to end. I didn't know how that was going to happen. There was a part of me that wanted the night to end the way they do in movies, a good-night kiss and more butterflies, but there was another side reminding me I hadn't had sex in months, and even longer for good sex. The mood was perfect, there was good music on the radio, he didn't switch to some corny love mix; he let his music play and eventually some set the mood songs crept in naturally, which told me he wasn't pressing me. Then the rain started out of nowhere. That was out of both our hands, that was the universe pushing our evening in the direction I was too scared to go.

As if the mood wasn't perfect, I loved the way he drove, one hand on the wheel, the other on my lap, but not too high so that I'd be creeped out, sitting leaned in his seat, his coat opened perfectly, with his fitted on. I'd be lying to myself if I didn't admit that I was turned all the way on. I'm pretty sure I could slide these ugly ass panties to the side and he'd never know, no shame, no foul. Then there's the where?

Do I really want to have sex with him at my girl's place. I know Sloane wouldn't care; she has told me more than a dozen times that it's my home too, but I couldn't. And I damn sure can't go back to his hotel room.

No Lyne'e, go home. When he pulled back up to our place, he showed no signs of pressure at all. He walked me to the door, shielding me and my edges from the rain with his coat and my hand in his. He was a gentleman, he lead the way and I gladly followed.

His Side ... The Growth

When Lyne'e left, she did her best to erase her footprints from my life; she cut off communication with me and our shared friends. She blocked me on her socials and my number from her phone. It was clear she didn't want to be bothered with me which I must admit hurt a little. I made some calls to find out exactly where she was staying, and the name Sloane kept coming up. Lyne'e has the worst taste in friends. All of them and Sloane was no exception. Sloane fucking hated me and I felt the same way about her ass.

I remembered Da'vere and Sloane hooked up a while back when she moved to Chicago but I remember him telling me it ended badly. Sloane might be an ass, but she was way out of his league, I never could figure out how he even convinced her to have drinks with him, let alone hit. If Sloane hated anyone more than she hated me it was Da'vere. Getting them in the same room together was always like pulling a bank heist. If Lyne'e had to do it, she planned and planned, made sure not to sit them near each other, didn't tell one the other was coming, insisted they bring a date to keep them distracted. Me on the other hand, I didn't care that much. Sloane was a stuck up boogie brat who could stand to be knocked off her high horse every once in a while. If I knew she was going to be at an event, I made sure my boy brought his baddest bitch.

So when he went through his phone and gave me her number and address I couldn't do shit but laugh.

"What the fuck so funny"

"Yo wack ass, I thought you hated Sloane, yet you still got her info saved in yo phone?" I chuckled.

"Look nigga you want the number or not?" He joked, before sending me the contact. I knew Sloane had moved since they hooked up, so I didn't understand why he had the address to her new place. I wanted to ask more about it, but figured it was better if I didn't know. Maybe his ass is out here doing some light stalking, shit ain't my business.

When I returned to work, it was to find out that Teagan had stolen one of my big accounts. Which she could have only done if someone gave it to her, shit I was gone for three days. From the time that I walked into the office to the moment I left, the day seemed to drag. By lunch I had sat in on two long unnecessary meetings, with some of the dumbest companies in Illinois, but any business is good business I guess.

Neither company kept any real receipts and one actually had the nerve to ask if they could pay me off the books or get a "look out". As if this isn't one of the top investment firms in the country. People lose their careers for stupid shit like that. I could only imagine the type of things that went on in this man's practice and had it not been for the sheer fact that I was curious I would have never agreed to take their business.

Of course since I took some time off I had to put on for Irwin's ass when I got back. He had me running across town to his favorite Italian restaurant picking up his lunch and then sitting in on yet another meeting that had nothing to do with me. A meeting he could have taken, but he and Teagan Stolfi were too busy in a random, very last minute business lunch with a client. I sat across from Mr. and Mrs. Shrewmaker's, a very old couple who happen to own three extremely successful restaurants and a nightclub. All silently of course. The two reminded me of the type of people you have to show how to use a cell phone, not the type to own a nightclub. I tried my hardest to appear both interested in what they had to say and pleased to fill in for Mr. Irwin.

"You must be a pretty smart boy if the Big Boss allowed you to take a meeting with us in his place. We've been doing business with your boss for over thirty years, he was no older than you when we met him. So how can you help us?" The old man asked me as he walked around the office space looking at the pictures, plaques, degrees and awards on my walls. His wife silently observes from a chair that I keep in front of the window for when I want to overlook the busy streets and clear my head. Forcing a smile I leaned back in my chair and quickly reminded myself that not everyone shares my common sense and views. This couple had to be in their late seventies, I'm sure they had a gentle old black woman cooking and cleaning for them back in the day, hell they may have one now, so referring to men of my ethnicity as "boy" is common tongue with them. As aware of the ignorance transpiring all around me I was, I'm in no mood to entertain it. This clearly wasn't a meeting for me and quite frankly if Irwin thought fucking Teagan in a cheap hotel room was more important than dealing with these rude ass people, then I will not do it either.

"I'm not sure if you need my help or want it for that matter, but you requested this meeting and I'm sure there was something that you wanted to address, so if you could tell me how I can help you, I can tell you if I can be of assistance."

"And your boss, where is he this afternoon? When it comes to me or my money, I don't like feeling like I'm just being passed along like a dirty penny." Mr. Shrewmaker decreed as he made his way back to his seat.

"Mr. Irwin had an emergency meeting that he needed to attend, he expressed how much he hated missing this meeting as your time is important and asked that I step in. I am more than capable of helping you with whatever it is that you have in mind." Sitting up in my seat and trying not to offend his old ass. "Sir all I need from you would be for you to let me know what brought you in today. I see that this appointment was only just added to the books yesterday. Did something happen or are you expecting an immediate change in your financial needs?"

"I'd really rather speak with your boss, can you go call him?"

After a deep breath we stared at one another. Him thinking he intimidated me and me thinking this is how I'm going to lose my job. "Mr. and Mrs. Shrewmaker, Irwin asked that I take this meeting because of all the people in this firm I am the most capable of helping you. Now I do not think that I will be giving you a resume of why I am capable of helping you. I don't believe that will be necessary but what I will do is reschedule your meeting in hopes that Mr. Irwin can make time to help you. Now if you would excuse me, let me direct you to my assistant and she will get you a new appointment that best fits your needs."

I stood up from behind the desk and walked over to the door, holding it open so that they both could get the hell out.

"No, if your boss is truly unavailable then I guess you will do." He replied as he ignored my subtle request for him to leave then took a seat next to his wife.

"No, no. Stacey will reschedule your meeting. I have my own clients that actually want my assistance and I need to prepare for them. Now if you would excuse me, it was very nice to meet you."

Mrs. Shrewmaker was the first to take the hint. That or maybe the irritated look on my finely carved black face did it for her, either way she clutched her handbag, smiled and walked out of the office just as silently as she entered. Her husband not so much.

"You know boy, I have been in business with this firm longer than you have been alive I'm sure and I do not appreciate being dismissed." He said as he walked towards me adjusting the hat on his balding silver head.

"You know Mr. Shrewmaker, my mother raised me to be nothing but respectful when I encounter people, because you never know what their life story may be. She also raised me to see the beauty in people and not their physical appearance. From the moment you walked into my office you were condescending and disrespectful. You have been a client here for as long as I have been alive, so I ignored it. I hope to one day be as active in my business and financial affairs as you are in yours, when I do make it to your age, but when I do, I plan on treating the people that I come in contact with, with a little more respect than you did me today. I have no intention of speaking down to another man and referring to him as a "boy" the way you just did to me for the past ten minutes. But just so you know, for this firm. I have handled multiple accounts three times the size of yours. My degree and common sense has allowed me to help those accounts grow into even larger ones. That is why Irwin asked me to help you, because sir I know my shit. Now if you would excuse me." I finished right before I turned my back and closed the door in Shrewmakers face. I'm sure Irwin is going to go ballistic over how I handled his clients, but I am not seasoned enough to handle such disrespect.

After this shit with the Shrewmaker's, I'm done for the day, my head is not in the game at all. I needed a shower, some good food, good head and a warm body to lay with and talk about my day. I need Lyne'e.

I shut my computer down, set up the call forward on my office phone to ring to my cell phone and ran down the hall to the elevator. It was my first day back and all I've been doing is catching up on other people's problems. I've had very little time to focus on my own clients while Irwin and Teagan are out doing whatever in the meantime. The two must really think it's funny, I'm jumping through hoops trying to make a name for myself meanwhile my primary competition is a bitch with no real fucking education or training sucking her way up the chain. I can't compete with that. The irritation must have been set in stone across my face. I could feel my lips pressed so tightly together that my teeth may puncture straight through the skin as I looked up and saw the elevator doors finally opened and Irwin and Teagan stepped off.

Ain't this some shit. As Irwin offered a pointless excuse for his absence before I could even say a word I remembered how many times I had done the same thing to Lyne'e. I wonder if she knew I was lying too? Teagan stood a few steps behind Irwin, trying not to look in my direction and mindlessly pressing buttons on her phone. I guess the two were so busy in the elevator that neither noticed the faint lipstick stain on his earlobe or chin.

Here I am, going above and beyond, staying late and coming in early, buying expensive property trying to impress him by showing him I can be a man that he can respect and he's fucking the office whore. And to make matters worse he's giving the bitch accounts and projects that should be mine.

"Excuse me, I have a meeting that I must get to, but I'll fill you in on today's events when you have time." I replied, making sure he saw my eyes focused on the remains of Teagan around his neck. Before he could reply I stepped forward onto the elevator and pressed the "close" button.

My drive home was a silent one. I feel stupid for letting this hoe shit get to me, I'd never hate on a man for getting his, Teagan is a beautiful girl. Honestly, she has movie star written all over her. She's too short to be a model, plus the girl likes to eat. The one thing about her I like. Not only does she pick the best restaurants, but she actually eats. And it shows, she's small, but not a basic white girl small, she has a little booty and some hips. Well for her frame, she has something. I'm pretty sure she's all natural, aside from that nose, she's too young to have fake breast already. But her face, she's actually a pretty girl, she has beautiful deep set green eyes, an upturned nose and strangely beautiful lips. They're fuller than her counterparts, but not too full to make me think she's mixed with any of mine.

When she's not being a bitch, she seems like she could be cool. It's clear that when she's not at work, she's the "good time" girl, I see her at casual work events, she always has a beer in hand and flashing a big childlike smile. When she laughs she usually has the loudest laugh in the room and she puts her whole body into it. Personally I never find anything at work that fucking funny, but she and I come from two different worlds. She probably laughs that hard at friendly sit-comes with dry sarcastic jokes and over reactions, where I like my comedy real, with a few mama jokes and actually relatable. I completely understand why Irwin would fuck her, but that's it. Fuck her and move the fuck on. I'd never take Irwin as a man who mix business with pleasure, not to this extent.

I needed a moment to clear my head and prepare my mind for getting Lyne'e back. Today was the perfect example of why I needed her back. Not to impress Irwin, but for her finesse. She would know how to handle this situation with Irwin and she would give me some advice on how to get rid of Teagan's ass. For the first time I realized that this woman was a direct threat to my career. As long as she had her pussy in Irwin's face she may as well have her name on the letterhead, because she was now calling the shots.

I pulled into the driveway of my new home and turned off the engine. I looked around at my new neighbors, all peaceful, happy and smiling. This could be us. I waved to my next-door neighbors, Steve. *I think that's his name.* He was an older gentleman with a wife my age and a one-year-old son that is driving him crazy. I wouldn't be surprised if I came home and found that he killed the entire family including himself. He just looked like the type. My guess is he wanted the young hot pretty wife, but did not sign on for the kid. She was his new lease on life and he was her retirement plan while that kid her insurance. They've invited me over for dinner but I rather not get involved until I have my girl back.

I took a long shower and threw on some sweats and a t-shirt. When Lyne'e sees me, I want her to think that I was a broken man since she left and what better way to do that than looking like shit. Lyne'e is smart, she knew I would never walk around looking a mess if I were in my right mind. I shuffled some clothes around in the master bedroom and throughout the house so that when she walks in, she would think that I really needed her to keep me on track. The truth is, she's the messy one, she knows how to cook but she's really good at surface cleaning. Her mom had someone come in and clean twice a month, so all they really had to do was keep the house pretty as kids, where I've been cleaning with my mom since I was eleven years old. My mom did not play about keeping her house clean. Our chores were not gender or age-specific, she didn't care, her kitchen was going to be cleaned every night and her bathroom every morning. After I threw some dishes in the sink, I headed out the door, putting the address Da'vere gave me in my GPS and offered a little prayer that this works and I get my peaceful life back.

I knew it was Sloane's condo the moment I pulled up. Only her stuck up ass could afford to live in a place like this with a guard at the front gate. I had to talk fast and explain to the man that I was here as a surprise and even flash him the engagement ring so that he didn't call ahead to warn them. Plus, I'm sure that damn hundred dollar tip didn't hurt either.

I pulled into the spot next to Lyne'e new 2007 black Charger, when she bought the car she used the address at the apartment and they sent a delicious "Thank You" basket. I couldn't believe she bought a new car, she's always so cautious with her purchases. A Charger seems completely outside of her character, some nigga must have suggested it.

I pulled next to it and peered through the windows. I want to make sure I saw nothing crazy like a car seat or some nigga's jacket. It's only been three months, but I think I would fall out if I saw either. I let my window back up and thought about what I was going to say. I had this sound plan in my head of getting her back, but I never thought about what I would actually say to her. Before I realized it an hour had passed. I probably would still be in deep thought had it not been for the rain beating down on my windshield snapping me out of my daze.

I thought to myself. I'll wait until the rain lets up just a little, so that I don't look like a crazy person standing outside her door in the pouring rain trying to plead my case. This ain't a damn music video.

As I pull the key from the engine, I notice a black Range Rover pull up to the front door. It's too far to tell, but the passenger looks like Lyne'e. I turned my car off and waited only to see some fool jump out the driver seat and run over to the passenger door and let my woman out of his car. This must be the dread headed clown Da'vere saw her with at breakfast. I want to keep my calm but I can feel the blood in my body boiling. Terrified she might see me or my car, I duck down in my seat and watch as this nigga walks the love of my life to her front door holding her hand the entire way.

And her, I know that walk; I know that smile she keeps giving him, and I know that look on ol' boy's face. This muthafucka thinks he's getting ready to fuck my girl and his bitch ass couldn't be more fucking wrong. I'll be damned if I'm going to lose my girl and especially to this lame. Not after all we've been through. I could feel the anger set in and the jealousy running scared from sight. She is the future mother of my children, the woman I planned on spending the rest of his life with. Hell, she is the reason I bought this three hundred thousand dollar house and she is going to live in it and be happy with me. I put my phone in the passenger seat and got out of the car. I can see her eyes fixate on me as I approached the two just in time to ruin what ol' boy thought was going to be a goodnight kiss.

At this point I knew he didn't see me, but she did and the smirk on her face let me know all that I needed to know, she was mine. She never took her eye off of me but cautiously she stepped in front of her date as if her little frame could ever stop me if was to fuck him up.

I didn't come to fight, and as mad as I was I didn't come to argue, all I wanted was Lyne'e. And as long as dude stay in his place, the night will go smoothly and I won't have to whoop his ass.

"Lyne'e we need to talk." I announced not even acknowledging her wack ass date. I watched as he put his arm around her waist, pulled her to his side asking if she wanted him to leave and the shocked expression on his face as she nodded yes.

"I'll call you later, thanks. I had a great time." She smiled graciously as she leaned in and kissed him on his cheek. Clearly they aren't serious because if they were she would have told him about me and he would have known to get the fuck on when he seen me standing there. Dude was really trying my patience, he wrapped his hands around my woman's waist a little too slow and a little too close to her ass. Lyne'e wasn't crazy, she instantly swatted his hands away and pulled back. Me not killing his ass right in that moment let me know that I have grown as a man and that this is what I want. Her. Us.

We both watched him walk away before I spoke. I was pleasantly surprised that she let me say anything, clearly she has grown too because the old Lyne'e would have gone off on me for popping up on her.

"You look great." I professed.

"Thank you Anderson, what are you doing here?" She questioned.

"I needed to see you, I need to apologize for the way things are between us. It's not right and I know it's my fault."

"And it took you three months to realize that, what happened, your other girl tired of you?" Lyne'e retorted. I couldn't tell if she was joking or not.

"You know there is no other girl and if there ever was she would never be important enough to come between me and you." I watched as she rolled her eyes and searched for her keys in her purse. "Lyne'e I'm serious, I miss you. More than I ever thought I could. I let the money and my ego cloud my judgment. For a moment I forgot who I was and how I became who I am, baby I couldn't have made it here without you always having my back."

I knew she heard me, her big pretty brown eyes watered, but I knew her. She will not fold easily. I continued to express to her how much I love her and would do anything at that point to get her back. I even managed to muster up a tear or two just to really let her know I was serious. I meant every word, I would do anything to be with her and if this is the version of me she wanted, then this was the version that she would get.

Her Side... The Discovery

I listened to Anderson in complete, utter shock and disbelief, especially considering I've heard all of these things before. The part that shocks me the most is his obsequious approach. The genuineness and sincerity he's able to convey for his bullshit is astonishing. In all of our years together I can count on my hands how many times he apologized and how many times he would go right back to his shit the moment I let my guard down.

I laughed a little in my head as I watched him use his hands to really get his point across like he used to do when he was nervous, but the tears. The tears were new; they were flattering and really almost convincing. I had only seen him shed a tear over death or if he was in enough pain, but never to convey real life emotion. *Hmmm so he's not a sociopath after all.*

Thank God Sloane pulled up flashing the lights on us, bringing a swift end to this long and awkward silent stare. I waved my hand to let her know I was ok and watched her as she bustled up the walkway.

"Hello Sloane" Anderson sighed, looking anywhere but in her actual face.

"Hello Mr. Hobbs" Sloane replied as she hugged me, looking Anderson directly in his eyes. Sloane really hated him, but she wasn't one to pry and that's what I loved about her. She respected boundaries, both he and I respected her for that.

Once Sloane was inside Anderson gave me a card with an address engraved in gold letters.

"I don't want to hold you two up, it's rainy and cold out here. I've already ruined your little date." He added sarcastically. "But there is an address on the card, if you get time tomorrow after work I would love it if you could meet me here." He said holding my hand too long as he was giving me a business card. I rubbed my fingers over the letters gently, but never offered an answer. I can't imagine why I would meet him anywhere and it is just like him to assume that I have nothing to do, but come when he calls. "Good night Anderson." I smiled before turning to walk inside, halfway through the door I heard him call my name. I slowly turned my head to meet his eyes as he shouted "He was tall, but that's all he was... he ain't me." We both shared a smile before I turned and stepped into the house.

I wanted to put on my unbothered face because I knew Sloane was waiting for me, but I couldn't stop smiling. I missed him; I didn't know how much until this very moment. Just to hear his voice, always so calm and deep or to look into his eyes. Those eyes get me every time, so big and brown, and his lashes. It almost looked like they were actually catching the raindrops and holding on to each one for safekeeping. Those stupid beautiful lashes always make it so hard to stay mad at him. *Ugh,* I rolled my eyes at myself as I locked the door.

When I turned the corner there was Sloane with a glass of wine and a smile waiting.

"I called Keyla, but she didn't answer and I can't wait for her to call me back to hear this. So..." she asked, adjusting herself in her seat.

Sloane Albertelli had become one of my closest friends. We met in college; we shared a few friends and always ended up in some of the same small circles. She was smart and funny ironically, but she was also a complete bitch and somehow the combination made her even prettier. She was a hit with the guys but women hated her. The women that looked like her didn't want to be bothered, the ones that looked like me didn't trust her, but what I liked about her is she never seemed to care. The friends she has loved her and she loved us right back. I could call her at two in the afternoon or two in the morning, she would be ready with any shit that I was on, no questions asked. She was the actual definition of a ride or die friend.

Sloane was a curvy Italian girl with thick curly hair that she hated and always wore straight. She has a beautiful naturally sun kissed complexion that she often tanned. She loved to cook and has introduced me to the beauty in pasta and wine, but she lived in the gym. Sloane was the type of beautiful that was often intimidating and can be threatening, but it was natural. She used her emerald green eyes and thick Boston accent to get us into every hot spot in the city and when either one of those didn't work she just pulled out a crisp hundred-dollar bill and slid it to the bouncer.

Sloane is a corporate attorney, but that's expected. Her dad Dante Albertelli is one of the most successful real estate attorneys in Boston and her mom Maria Albertelli is a corporate attorney turned music executive for a famous label. She was an only child who was to inherit a wealthy estate, but she wanted to earn and keep her own money. She is by definition a daddy's girl and even though he claims not to spoil her; he pays for her apartment, and her first Maserati, her Jeep she pays for.

Outside of her taste in men, she has never done a thing wrong in his eyes. Sloane exclusively dated black men, something that drove her family crazy. Her dad wanted a big Italian family, with the exception of his mid western fake southern belle second wife CiCi. For years I could not figure out if Sloane's taste in men was to spite her dad or that old wives' tale "once you go black" but either way every guy she brought home visibly disgusted her dad. Yes he liked me, but then again I couldn't get his daughter pregnant.

I smiled and set my purse down on the couch behind me "So what?"

"Don't play dumb with me, when I talked to you last you were on your way out with that tall and sexy adonis of a man, I get home and find you with the snake. What the hell Lyne'e? Talk!"

I tried to explain it to myself so that I could explain it to my friend but none of it made any sense. Why, of all nights, I finally get out of my way and agree to a date with Jamal, only for Anderson to show up. Sloane and I sat up talking about our days over a few bottles of wine before falling asleep on the couch.

The next morning I couldn't get Anerson out of my head. I wanted so badly to be angry at him, to hold on to the hurt and not let him get into my head, but him in the rain made it hard. We've been together through more rainy moons than I could count. Those rainy nights were some of our hottest. In college we didn't live together so sleeping alone or on the phone during a storm was easy. Moving back home with him, being stuck in a hot apartment with no roommates to disturb us and nothing to do with our time but get lost in each other, that was hard. We weren't even a month into our new place when it rained for four straight days and for four straight days Anderson and I made a new name for what we had done. It was so hot that we used our tub as our own personal pool. I layed naked in his arms for hours. His breath on my neck, his arms around my breast, waist, inside of me. His firm dick tapped my spine while he told me about his childhood. When we weren't in our pool we were sitting under the front window, sweat covering our bodies trying to abstain from any form of frolicing long enough to cool off. Which never lasted long because the moment our eyes met or the slightest sliver of our skin touched we were back at it. There was a time I couldn't go a day without kissing him, kissing his lips made him pull me tight into his arms, the moment I felt his chest against mine I knew what was coming next. His erections always seem to come with a heat seeking superpower that had no problem finding the warmest part of me. For years it didn't matter where we were if the wind blew in the right direction, that missile always hit its mark.

I needed to get this man out of my head so that I could keep him out of my heart. I swiped my badge and sashayed into the office on a mission. I was all too determined to make up for last night. If I was going to let Anderson work his magic on me and I fall back into some stedford-like utopia, I needed to rid myself of this feeling. Just to remind myself that I did something that wasn't right, that I didn't spend my entire life with one man and one man only. I want to be able to teach my future daughter to live her life, to love often and actually have a frame of reference for comparison. I know me and I know Anderson. He has already worked up a speech and I have already accepted the bullshit that he will be serving. I know he's smart enough to learn from his mistakes if he showed up here. I know I will be Mrs. Lyne'e Hobbs, but before I walk down that road I need to feel what it is like to be adorned by a man such as Jamal Wells. I need to know I'm not missing out on anything.

Deep in thought, I walked right past the young man calling my name a little too loudly and disturbing my thought process. I turned to face my new assistant and without even knowing it I was giving him the look of death. Poor thing, he couldn't have been but a few years older than I was and yet he was my assistant. He was smart and attentive, but he was interrupting my impure thoughts yammering on about meetings and messages.

By the time we reached my office I had heard about the three meetings I have for the day, the lunch I absolutely need to attend with our legal team and the dozens of reports that apparently I have to review or the world would end. My new position is Enterprise Operational Risk Analyst. It was something the firm was leaning into, so not only was this new for me it was new for everyone.

By the end of the day I was so tired that my thoughts were even over it. When I wasn't thinking about my messed up life, I was solving work problems, when I wasn't solving work problems, I was a sounding board for future work problems. I had reviewed so many loans, accounts and reports that my eyes were starting to criss cross. I was in no mood to play games, to flirt, hell I was too tired to smile let alone entertain Anderson. Trying to look sexy this morning, I put on the wrong heels so now my feet are on fire. I pulled my hair up in a very messy bun and whatever makeup that I thought I had on, had left the building hours ago. I couldn't think of anything I'd rather do than take a hot shower and curl up next to a steaming hot pizza.

The closer we were to five, the softer the office chatter had become. The phone calls had tapered down for the day, the printers were finally slowing down and the smell of burnt popcorn was finally beginning to fade away. In order to finish these reports I'd need to walk a hundred miles down the road to the good printer because the one by my office was down again. The company had apparently been out to fix this damn machine five times this year, six if you count their scheduled trip tomorrow. The one good printer was down the hall and these six hundred dollar pumps had served their purpose and long gave up on me. All I needed was one color copy of one report and of course it couldn't wait until morning according to Collette. Thank goodness the people on this floor run out of here at exactly five o'clock like their lives depend on it. The floor was finally deserted, I should be able to make it down the hall barefoot without appearing to be some country bumpkin. I hit print on my computer and quietly tiptoed down the hall, with extra papers in one hand and looking through my text messages with the other.

" ... I'm assuming that was your ex you mentioned, does this mean you are off the market again, or do I still have a chance to..." J 8:17 am

"... A chance to... what?" Lynee 8:23 am

I was so focused on my phone that I didn't see the printer before running into it. Something told me to look around and of course I found a few people still in the conference room laughing and waving their hands for me to come in. I gave the room my gracious smile as I stepped into the room, hoping that no one would notice my bare naked toes.

"It's so late, what are you guys still doing here, I thought I was alone?" I uttered low and shyly.

"We were just finishing up, about to head out for a drink, care to join us" Cliff asked in his usual creepy tone. Cliff is the office sleaze; everything he said had a dirty undertone to it. I have made it my life's mission not to ever get stuck on the elevator or in the parking complex with him for fear he had bodies in his trunk or something.

"I'm sure Lyne'e has better things to do, like shoe shopping, than to be bothered with us!" Tyra interrupted me long enough for me to notice she was sitting side by side with Jamal, a little closer than I felt she needed to be. I hated Tyra, she was a pretty girl who titties sagged and flopped from side to side whenever she moved, a questionable weave and a shitty attitude who hit on every man that walked into the office. I didn't like her from the day we met, I guess she saw me as competition as if I wanted any of the men that worked for this firm. She was too busy trying to land a man while I'm trying to figure out how I could take over. We may both be single black females, but we have absolutely nothing in common.

I swallowed the urge to roll my eyes at both Cliff and Tyra and answered politely before exiting the room "No, I'm going to head home, open up a bottle of wine and look over these reports, but you guys have a good time and drink for me." Once safely in my office and back in my shoes I began packing up my things so that I could get on the elevator before the late-night crowd and before Cliff. I was all too ready to leave for the day as it is and now after seeing that Jamal was not dead just not responding to my text message I was really ready to go home.

Maybe seeing Anderson was too much for him and now he wasn't interested any longer. That's fine, I just wish I didn't feel so desperate. I clicked off the light to my office, still lost in my thoughts or in my feelings. *What the hell is wrong with me today?* I just felt stupid. As I pushed the button to the elevator, I realized I am now talking to myself, aloud. I peered around hoping that I am alone with my own crazy, only to see Jamal standing in silence watching me. Our eyes met, and a smile stretched across my face. *Shit, stop smiling.* Thank goodness he reciprocated my reaction. My smile instantly became a nervous impulse.

"Hello beautiful, I was hoping I would catch you before you skirted off."

"Oh really, what can I do for you?"

"You could let me take you out for a bite to eat. I'm starving and I don't know this area that well. Plus, I would love your company." He asked, stepping inside the elevator behind me. This man was all kinds of sexy, and I was a bundle of emotions and all of them triggered by the mere thought of him.

"Sure, but just you and I right? I'm really not in the mood for a crowd."

"Just me and you. I have no intentions on sharing you with anyone. And I do mean anyone."

I blushed at his implication, I'm sure he is referring to Anderson popping up last night. And as far as I can see in the near future, sharing me is the last thing he has to worry about. I've been all his since the moment I laid eyes on him. I just hope he's worth the commitment.

The elevator doors slowly closed just in time for Tyra to come sashaying down the hall. As she was yelling out to hold the door, I was pressing the close button. I'm glad she saw us together, maybe now she'd sit her hot ass down somewhere and stop sniffing up behind my future ex. To assure just a little bit of privacy, we took separate cars and left the parking structure at two different exits. The last thing I want is to be the new girl and office gossip.

We met at the light around the corner and I followed him to a little Italian restaurant about twenty minutes away. Once inside he requested a private booth in the back of the restaurant where we could be alone in our conversation without constantly looking over our shoulders for coworkers or nosy lookers. He ordered us a few appetizers, a bottle of wine and dessert. We joked about a few people around the office and he told me about his life back home. I shared a little more about my life and what brought me here but nothing about our evening was more delightful than laughs. Jamal is a very funny man, but not too silly. He has an ironic sense of humor that I enjoy. He has long dreads that he kept pulled back in a ponytail while working and smooth dark brown skin paired perfectly white a Colgate smile. His eyes were just as dark as his skin and his hands looked like they were made for hard work.

I took a large sip of my wine and worked up the nerve to ask him about his text from earlier that morning. It had a very vague open ending.

"So what did you mean and why so vague?"

He smiled and replied, "Whatever your mind was thinking, that's what I was implying."

When the smile on my face faded, Jamal leaned across the table and placed both my hands in his. His hands are hard and strong, with his thumb gently racing the palms of my hands and his eyes staring into mine, for that moment he owned me. The restaurant was busy but our moment was quiet, deep and intense. Finally he broke our moment

"Lyne'e tell me something, what are you looking for, for real? I don't think I can give you anything serious with us living states apart but I really want to spend more time with you. Maybe I'm looking too far ahead, but I think I really like you."

Never taking his eyes from mine he licked his lips and continued "I know I've been pursuing you hard for a few months now and before you gave me absolutely no play, but then all of a sudden something changed. I finally get you to agree to go out with me and your ex pops up. It's none of my business, I guess I need to know what is going on with you two. At least so I can know where I stand. I really like you, I think you're smart, beautiful and sexy as fuck. If I'm being honest there aren't too many days lately that the thought of you doesn't end in a long cold shower or an extra rep or two at the gym. I just need to know where you and I stand, if it's physical and you are just using me to get over him, then cool, trust me, I know a few tricks that'll make you forget that nigga name." He laughed. "But if you think you may want something more, if any part of you thinks about me like I think about you, you've got to let me know. I'll make arrangements and we can figure this thing out."

I don't know what made me laugh, rather it was seeing him blush his way through his speech or the tickle from his lips on my hands, but I was giggling like a schoolgirl at the wrong time.

He continued "I want you, I want all of you. I actually have a long list of things I want to do to you. I just need you to tell me yes and I'll take it from here. Or did your ex showing up ruin any chances that I have or had?"

My entire life has been carefully calculated, well thought out steps. Even as a teenager I was not impulsive. Just once I wanted to live in the now, be young and free to do whatever I want and to make my own mistakes. At twenty-six I had been with two men and neither one of them gave me this feeling that I get when I simply hear Jamal speak. He spoke with a street accent, even when he was being professional.

Something about his energy made me feel safe, from what I don't know, but I know when he's around I feel like a damsel in distress and I liked it. I wanted everything that he'd mention; I wanted to be the focal point of his attention mentally and physically. Even as he spoke all I could do was watch his big pillow-like lips slowly form shapes that I instantly wanted all over my body. He is talking about something serious and all I could think is I how him to fuck me. I know Anderson and I are written, but shit right now?

All the love and loyalty that I have shown Anderson, I needed to show to myself. For once I was going to be loyal to the only person in my life that matters. I needed to be loyal to myself.

There are fireworks going off inside of me and they are all shining bright over the possibility of Jamal and I. I pulled one hand from his powerful grip and signaled for the waitress to bring the check. The waitress must have known the night I had in store because she walked over promptly and set the bill on the table. I glanced at the bill $128.97, went into my purse and pulled out three very crisp fifty-dollar bills, gave them to her and without saying a word took the last shot of cognac from Jamal glass and asked if he were ready to leave. On the outside the move was bold but on the inside the cognac was burning a hole in my chest and not my nerves.

He cleared us a path through the crowded restaurant; the air was filled with loud bursts of laughter and cheers but all I could focus on was how I felt in his hand as he led. Once outside he gave our tickets to the valet and we stood in silence. I could feel Jamal staring down at me but I was too nervous to turn and look his way. The chill in Chicago's night air sends a shiver down my spine but nothing like the one I felt when Jamal placed his hand on my back to usher me inside of my car. The shiver was far from comparison to the feeling I felt as he leaned in and kissed me before closing the door. This was not the soft peck he placed on my cheek the night before, this kiss was transcending. Shit it transcended me right out of my panties. Suddenly I could easily see us saying fuck a bedroom, lets pull these cars over and do this right on the side of the road. He left a tingle in my thighs and his taste on my tongue. My heart was beating three times its usual rate, and I was literally out of breath, but I liked it. Who needs my morning run, what I needed was him at the first sight of dawn and I would be alright.

I guess he didn't want this night to end again with a bitter ex popping up; he asked that I follow him, and at that point I would have followed him almost anywhere. He closed my car door, stepped around to his car and drove off doing at least 55 mph. Following his rented Cadillac I turned my radio all the way up, not wanting the silence to change my mind in any way. I plugged my phone up and played my slow grooves playlist. The problem is, this is a playlist that Anderson and I used to listen to and it could not be the soundtrack for tonight. I skipped forward only to find another song that reminded me of him. Clearly music wasn't working. I see Anderson's face and smile and now I hear him saying "he ain't me".

So I turned the music down and called Kim, if anybody can help me get my mind right it was Sloane.

..."hey, are you at home?" I asked loudly.

"Yeah just walked through the door, what time are you coming? I rented a movie and got a bottle of Tequila. I don't want to hear about work. I just want to sit on the couch, eat junk food and watch Boris Kodjoe," Sloane declared as she crunched on chips.

"I'm going to have to take a rain check. I think I have something better to do."

"What could you possibly have better to do then spend the night chilling and drinking with the only person to love you like I do?"

"Jamal Wells." I answered like a giddy schoolgirl.

"Shut up, that tall fine ass man from last night? You??? Wait a minute is Lyne'e there? Can I speak to my friend because the Lyne'e I know would never say she is 'doing' anyone let alone actually do someone as sexy as a Mr. Jamal Wells." Sloane laughed.

Sloane 'slaughter made me a little more comfortable. "So here is what you're going to do. A man that big has to be that big everywhere. I don't think you're ready for that just yet, get him on his back and ride him like yo ass is going to win the Nobel Peace Award for it. Do you hear me? If he knows what he's doing he'll throw it back at you, if he does not, do not let him up until you get your second one. You need this.

"You know I hate you right?" I laughed.

"No you don't, that's why you called me. Now if it gets really good and you think you're ready, suck his dick til he feels like he has died and gone to heaven. Right when he's reaching to grab on to the pearly gates and then fuck him until he's calling for his momma. You make a man cry for his momma, then you have changed his life."

I laughed so hard at her the tears in my eyes had almost blinded me. "The point that I'm making is, tonight don't be you, be me. Better yet be that nasty bitch Nessa from English 101, remember her? Yeah be her." I laughed until all the nerves were gone and all I wanted to do was make my friend proud. For once I wanted to have a story to tell Sloane that would make her blush like her stories always did to me.

I ended the call once we pulled in front of The W. Since I had to approve the accommodations for the Canon Pharms trip; I knew that this room was not on the approved list for hotels that our company paid for. This place is far from the $60 a night group rate rooms that I approved. As the valet opened my car door, I found myself looking around feeling some form of shame. I gave the valet my keys while wondering where the hell did his hotel come from? Suddenly it occurred to me Jamal is a very attractive man, I'm sure I am not the only woman in Chicago that finds him attractive, maybe this was his weekend pied-à-terre. As I took his awaiting hand, I knew there was no hiding my thoughts behind my expression. I could feel my brow wrinkled and my side eye growing more and more vivid. The nervous feeling was back, but this time it wasn't alone. I was a ball of emotions. I almost felt like a virgin.

Like my first time I didn't know what to expect, and I wanted to turn and run. Why were we here instead of the room that the company paid for? Should I be flattered or offended? How many women had he brought here? Am I the first of many or the last of a dying breed? If this is how he entertained, can I keep up? I was shaking but this time it wasn't the night air; it was fear coursing through me. I noticed the fancy paintings and detailed architects, the plush but modern furniture providing the main lobby with a chic and welcoming feeling. I tried to distract myself by focusing on the small talk around me, but the sound of the strangers' voices were not as loud as the voices in my own head. We walked past the front desk where a pretty dark-haired young lady smiled and nodded her head at Jamal who offered a kind smile in return. He stepped with confidence as usual while I exhibited a predetermined walk of shame. I began to wonder if the smile between the concierge and Jamal was a private joke; her noticing that he had another victim and him laughing acknowledging that he indeed did. We said nothing all the way up to the twentieth floor. The only communication between us two were light squeezes of my hand in his and a brief kiss across my knuckles.

I took a deep breath as the red light on the keypad of the door flashed green. As he held the door open I just stood there, frozen in that one spot. I knew I needed to step over the threshold and into the room but I was too nervous. Nope, this is not nervous, this feeling is good old fashion fear. I've been with two men, one who just told me he loved me, well maybe not me but my voicemail. And now here I am getting ready to make those two, three and I'm not sure if I can. I could hear the sound of my own heart beating in my ear.

He must have sensed my hesitation because he stepped back outside the door. "Hey, we don't have to do this, just kissing you tonight was enough for me. I don't want you to do anything you aren't ready for."

The sincerity in his voice touched me. This was what I wanted to do, but now I'm not sure if I know how. As he stood before me, just as tall, just as handsome and somehow even sexier than before things came into focus. This is what I wanted.

"I'm fine, just a little nervous."

"Baby you never have to be nervous with me. What changed?" He asked while swooping my hair out of my face.

"I don't know exactly, maybe it is this hotel. This isn't the room we provided for your company. Is this where you bring all of your women when you are here on business?" Even as I said the words, I wanted to take them back. I don't think I really want to know the answer to my question. And seeing how he's laughing I really don't think I want him to answer me now.

"There are no other women, there is only you. Every time I visit Chicago it's just you. When you agreed to have dinner with me I called my brother back home and asked him to book me a room for the weekend here. I didn't want anyone in our business and I know you have a roommate. I wanted you alone and too myself, especially after your ex made a special appearance last night."

I felt stupid. He did the right thing; I hadn't even thought about his coworkers at the other hotel. A rush of relief washed over me.

"So..." He asked.

I was too embarrassed to say a word, so I let my actions at the moment speak for me. Grabbing the lapels of his jacket I pulled him down close enough for our lips to meet. Once I was firmly wrapped in his arms and kisses, I felt free. No more nervous flutters and scary thoughts. My restraints had broken. He held me close in his arms and kissed me deeply, my mouth welcoming his as I pushed my body further into his. He pushed my head over to the side with his and sucked my neck as if we were filming a love scene in a teenage vampire movie. I could feel fireworks bursting in my veins and an urgency in my pelvis. The ambers from those fireworks he had started before we created fire deep inside of me, my body was blazing and the only thing that could put me out was him.

I reluctantly pulled away long enough to walk inside of the room. Jamal standing behind me running his hands around my waist, one up to my breast and the other between my thighs forcing my knees to buckle at his touch. He grabbed the top of my pelvis as if he was trying to pull it off and take it with him all the while focusing his thumb on my clitoris. Tilting my head back I found his mouth with mine and kissed him, mirroring his aggression and passion. Once inside, the door closed and I don't remember my feet actually touching the grown. He slammed me against the wall by the door, then we stumbled to a table where he sat me on the edge and placed his hands between my legs just high enough for his thumb to lightly grace the peak of my thighs. The sensation was so overwhelming, forcing a natural arch in my back causing my breast to rise to a perfect angle for Jamal's mouth to meet. As he nibbled the apex of my breast, I could feel my legs stiffening and my body rocking.

I wanted this man so bad. He lifted me off the table and carried me over to the bed. I could still taste the cognac on his tongue and smell his cologne in the air. It was an intoxicating fragrance that I think will haunt my dreams. Once he laid me down in the middle of the suit king-size mattress, he stood there and stared at me. Our eyes spoke words to one another that our mouths could never murmur. He pulled my heels off one by one caressing each foot, staring me in the eyes the entire time. The moment was so sexy.

His hands moved quickly up my legs, he placed my right thigh in both his hands and messaged it, gentle long strokes up and down. My back arching without warning, my nipples perking up crying out for his attention while the heat coming from between my thighs was undeniable. Focusing on my eyes he kneeled down over me and positioned his face between my legs. I could hear him moan as he took a deep breath in, breaking our eye contact just that one time to close his eyes and frolic in the moment. Over my now drenched panties he nibbles, a sweet interlude as to what's to come, sending me sky high. I was so turned on. His every touch was by definition perfect.

Just as I was getting into the moment he leaned up and kissed me before walking into the bathroom. I could hear the water rushing from the shower and then him calling out for me.

Still lying in the position he left me, I closed my eyes and squeezed my pelvis as tight as I could. I didn't want the feeling clawing inside me to get out and leave for good. After a few moments I decided that pouting would not get me anywhere and got up to meet him in the bathroom. To my surprise, he has lit a few candles and bath water running. I giggled embarrassingly, I couldn't hold it in nor hide the pleased expression on my face. This is the type of thing you hear about in old love songs or in romantic movies, never in a million years had I ever really expected to have it done for me.

I shushed the voice in my head once more and focused on the boyish look on Jamal's face. As shocked as I was, I didn't think he may be feeling the same.

I offered a smile hoping to ease his mind and assure him I loved all of this. There was music playing which I couldn't hear from the bed, the relaxing notes of jasmine and lavender in the air and him in a towel.

I could see why all of his suits were tailored, his body was in even better shape than I'd imagine. I almost feel intimidated, I don't know rather than to take off my clothes or drop and give him twenty. Everything on his body was cut and shaped exactly where it should have been, he even has tattoos. I would have never expected tattoos. His dreads now out of their ponytail falling perfectly over his shoulders and down his back was the perfect icing on the perfect cake.

"So this happened fast, what is all this, and when did you set it all up?"

"When my brother made the arrangements, I requested in detail what I wanted." he replied while slowly walking over to me.

"What made you so sure I wouldn't back out?"

"Wishful thinking I guess. You have no idea how bad I want you." He whispered in my right ear while pulling me into the bathroom and backing me up against the sink. His soft lips feel like pillows kissing on mine, touching my skin, biting me, and caressing me all while unzipping my skirt and sliding it down my thighs. This man is smooth. Goose bumps spread over me as he removed my panties taking each foot out one at a time. Once I stood there completely nude from the waist down, his voice low and faint "you are so fucking beautiful" was the last thing I heard before my own moans reverberated over the bathroom walls.

His lips sucking at the heart of my femininity, my body being supported by our weight on the sink and his left hand while the two fingers on his right climbed deep inside of me adding to my demise. His hand and his tongue worked together like a hit man on a secret mission to bring me down. Each stroke followed by a powerful flick of the tongue building these minor explosions inside of me. Each explosion forced down my internal walls destroying the structure that is me until there was nothing left to protect. I began falling apart. My hands now on his head trying to force his face from my thighs hoping if he was away, this joyful agony would be as well. I cam again. Me screaming out his name while an ocean of me washed over his face, his hands and then down his arm. I screamed louder, a sound I had no memory of ever making before while my grip around the crown of his head tightened. I was torn. I knew I didn't want him to stop, but I wasn't sure that I could take any more.

He set back on the tub, his eyes back fixated on me and mine trying to focus on anything but him. My legs felt weak, but I could still stand. My chest rising with every breath and collapsing beats later. I want to address a question that he asked me earlier, but I didn't want to spoil our night. That voice in my head was screaming no, don't do it, but I knew I couldn't fully enjoy him or this moment if I didn't tell him how I felt truthfully.

"Right now I'm in a crazy space, and to answer your question from dinner, yes I want you, but no I don't want a commitment. I've been in a relationship since I was eighteen years old and I'm not completely sure that I'm ready to be in another one."

Jamal looked puzzled, I could see his eyes dancing over my body as if I had said nothing. After a few moments of uncomfortable silence he spoke, "your skin is so soft and silky." He said running the back of his hand up my side to my breast. "Your breasts are perfectly shaped, are they yours?" He asked, never looking me in my face. "You are truly one beautiful woman, do you know that?"

I decided to skip his line of questioning and continued "right now I feel like I need this, like I need you, but if you are looking for anything more out of me at this point in my life, it may be best if we didn't do this. I'm not saying that I don't like you, because I do. I really do, but emotionally I am a mess right now."

He finally broke his stare from my shivering body and looked deep into my eyes and smiled. "I want you. So whatever that means to you right now, then that's what it is. We can take this as slow or as fast as you need to."

His words mean everything to me, I didn't know how he was going to take what I had to say and most of all; I didn't think he would be so accepting of it. A childlike smile spread across my face as I leaned down and pulled Jamal closer to me and let him have his feel of me. I unwrapped his towel and checked him out all over, I even twirled my finger in the air signaling for him to turn around so that I could see the entire package that was Jamal Wells. I was unequivocally impressed. If the look on my face didn't convey my enthusiasm I'm sure my nipples piercing through my bra and shirt did. I ran my fingers through the little hair on his chest, stomach and down to his well-manicured manhood. My eyes widened, and the butterflies were back the moment I felt it growing even bigger in my hand.

I removed my shirt and bra and stepped inside the perfectly run bathtub. We talked as if we've known each other our entire lives, played silly little love games, shared soft kisses and talked some more.

The moment was perfect, if only for this one night, this one time I had a perfect night.

Jamal stood up and reached for my hand, I stared at him, all of him. Water dripping off his amazing physique onto the floor pooling at his feet. I obliged. He wrapped a towel around his waist bringing an end to my little peep show and then draped a towel around me and led me into the bedroom. After he wiped every speck of water off of my body, paying very close attention to all my delightful spots he kissed me on the forehead and went back into the bathroom. Suddenly tonight seemed real. There was nothing else to do but make love. My heart started racing, and this rush came over me. I wasn't nervous or scared even, I was anxious. My stomach felt like it was ready to fall right out of me and I could feel my skin heating up. My mouth was watering and something inside of me was vibrating.

I was becoming annoyed. I had waited all of my life for a night like this and this urgency inside of me was not willing to wait any longer. I got up from the bed and wrapped the towel around me.

I shook my head 'no' disagreeing for once with the voice in my head and let my towel hit the floor. I walked lightly on my tiptoes to the bathroom calling out for him with every other step.

"Are you looking for me?" He asked, stepping into the doorway.

"I thought you had run off and left me. You had me thinking that this really wasn't what you wanted." I said with a salacious wink and a smile. With no warning whatsoever he reached his hands in between my thighs and pushed his fingers inside of me bringing the big girl inside of me to a whimpering child. Once he had me in his hands, firmly he pressed me against the wall and dug deeper finding my A-spot then G-spot and owning it. His fingers flickered back and forth making me move to his rhythm and forcing an orgasm where I thought there was none. My head tilted down and my mouth fixed in an ahh position. He ripped open a gold wrapped condom, spitting the wrapper on the floor and placing himself securely inside of me. Baiting another explosion inside of me. One leg thrown around his thighs and another barely touching the ground, my body welcomed every thrust and even managed to throw some back. I was new to this level of emotion but not new to this game we were playing. My nails digging into his shoulder and his into my hips, knocking me hard against the cool wall which was no match for this inferno burning inside of my body falling forward onto his. I scream as he slams into me, hitting spots I had no idea were in his reach to hit. His lips finally found mine, he thrust his tongue into my mouth causing me to lose my breath.

"Is this mine?" he whispers in my ear and slams my body down harder onto his dick. "Say it baby, tell me it's mine." I'm speechless. My mouth refused to close long enough for me to utter a word so what came out was some weird moan. "I need to hear it, baby. Tell me. You can't cum until I know you're mine." He whispered in between slight nibbles on my earlobe.

From that moment each thrust was harder, slower, somehow deeper. Without any approval from me, my mouth moaned the magic words "It's yours." Those words must have been his cheat code, from the moment the words left my lips I swear it felt like he grew bigger as he pounds harder and harder on this barrier inside of me. I moaned louder as he hit it again, louder as this tension in my body builds, I could feel it in my fingers, my thighs, my back, my inside is going to explode. I could feel the ground under me shaking, I held on tight and like the ball dropping at midnight on New Year's Eve I exploded. Balloons and confetti falling from my ceiling, feeling me with pride, cheerfulness, pleasure. Lord yes, the pleasure. It was like I had awakened from a twenty-six-year coma, completely aware of my time in space and feeling myself for the first time ever. I could hear, I could see, I could taste pleasure and it was good.

Hours later, the only movement that my body could produce was an intense shaking. I had spent the past two hours on my knees, on my back, on my stomach, hell on my shoulder, I had been tangled in positions that I didn't even know I could fit in. And with no warning when he should have been as tired as I am, he rolled me on my back and slowly slid inside of me, gripping my waist and moaning out in between every long hard stroke. I bit my bottom lip and tried my best to match his stroke, guiding him into our own orgasmic space in time where he has sent me over and over tonight. When I felt him losing his wits and ready to end this final round, I pushed him over and climbed on top of him burying my feet into the bed bending my legs and forming a squat like position on top of him; I clenched my walls tightly around his dick and pounced up and down until I saw his eyes close and his mouth open. No actual words escaped his lips, but when I heard him let out a noise that I had become all too familiar with I knew I had him. His body tightened underneath mine like a surfboard and me on top riding him into the waves of me. My explosion was a little one in size but huge for my ego.

Now for once tonight he was the one shaking and speechless underneath me. I was the victor of this round and not a moment too soon. I was exhausted. My body fell over next to his, as if someone had shot me. He must have been just as tired because the only sound filling our room was the sound of him snoring.

Awakened by my internal alarm clock and small rays of sunlight, I awaken with a smile plastered on my face. And a bit of drool on my cheek. Before turning over to face the man that has changed my life, I quickly wiped my face and pulled my hair behind my ears. To my surprise, he was still asleep and with the condom on to boot. I guess last night was a big night for him as well. I softly got out of the bed and tiptoed to the bathroom. For the first time in a long time I was pleased with the lady staring back at me. She looked happy and rested. I turned on the water to muffle the sound of me peeing that always seems embarrassing to me. I am in no condition to go anywhere, let alone for my morning run. Shit, my legs still feel like wet noodles and my body feels like I've been working out. All I want to do is take a hot shower and crawl back into the bed. Hell, Jamal doesn't even have to be in it. I want to sleep, ugly, loud and wild. I want to stretch out with my mouth open and call the hogs as my dad would say. And if Jamal is here, then I would have to be pretty and sleep like the women do in movies. Nope, I need to get out of here and to my own bed.

I washed my hands and used the complimentary mouthwash left by the hotel staff. The only thing that could ruin this perfect experience is morning breath. Before exiting the bathroom I took one more look at myself in the mirror loving this new me. The old me would never walk around naked and be this comfortable, but this new me, is confident and comfortable in my skin.

I crept back to the bed, trying not to awake my sleeping soldier of love feeling the pain in my every step. My body was the battlefield at which an orgasmic war was at fault, I may have lost the battle but I proudly claim victory to the war. I was sore in some places and numb in others, and when I should feel enervated, I felt powerful. I have never felt a wave of emotion and strength before. There were two things I was unequivocally sure about, first I wanted Jamal, right here, right now even more than I did last night and secondly, there was no going back to who I was before. My mind has been blown and once a bell has been rung, you cannot un-ring it.

I glanced over at the clock on the nightstand realizing I still had to get ready for work. I couldn't decide on another round of Jamal or make it to work on time. My thoughts interrupted by the abrupt snoring of the man laying beside me, I looked around for my phone hoping to catch Sloane before she left the house, maybe she could bring me some clothes.

"... Hey, I'm going to be running late for work and I still have on the same clothes from last night. Be my knight and shining armor and bring me something to wear to the office before you go in." Lyne'e 5:13 am

"Who could you possibly be texting this early?" Jamal asked, laying on his side, completely nude, dick hard and smiling at me.

"Well, good morning to you too."

"It's not a good morning yet, com here." He demanded as he pulled me by my waist to his side of the bed. He rolled over on top of me pulling the covers over us with one hand and reaching onto the nightstand with the other lightly caressing a spot he had begun to know all too well. Here he is, on his knees hovering over me using those big brown eyes to stare deep down into mine causing me to melt under his glare. I reach my hand up and caress his chest, outlining the ink of his tribal tattoo.

He leans his head down and kisses my fingers. He doesn't stop me as I place my fingers in his mouth, in fact he welcomes it and invites the other. With his eyes still burning into mine I can hear the condom wrapper rip and moments later I can feel him inside of me. I pull my fingers from his wanting mouth and place them above my head gripping the pillow. I want to look away, suddenly I feel shy, aware that it's no longer dark in our love nest and that he can see me, the real me, by the light of day. I quickly look away embarrassed by what my sex faces must look like to him. He slows his rhythm and turns my head back to his. "You are so beautiful, don't you dare turn away from me." Hesitantly I do as I'm told. "I could look into those eyes every day. Your beautiful Lyne'e do you know that?" His question couldn't have come at a worst time. I was vulnerable and open, in more ways than I care to think about. Thankfully, he must have super powers and could read my mind because he didn't wait for a response. Instead, he placed my leg over his shoulder and dug himself as deep as he could inside of me. I could feel that good'ol feeling again, he's spinning me.

I enjoyed Jamal one more time in the shower before I left to meet Sloane at her office. Thank goodness it wasn't too far from mine. I couldn't believe the last twenty-four hours of my life. Here I am standing in front of Sloane 'soffice in the same clothes as last night but wearing them completely different. I felt anew.

Sloane walked up to me carrying her overnight Chanel bag and a cup of coffee smiling from ear to ear.

"Now I know you don't have time right now, but if you don't call me by noon, I will be in your office in that little black chair waiting to hear all the tea honey. I want to know it all." She said smiling and giving me the bag and the well needed cup of coffee.

"You know you get on my nerves right?"

"I'm fine with that, as long as you tell me what got into you last night. Look at you, glowing and shit. Call me as soon as you get to your office. I can't wait til noon." Sloane said laughing as she hugged me and turned to walk off.

Once in the office I went to the gym in the basement and got dressed there. I didn't want to risk anyone seeing me and my hoe bag in the office. And of course Sloane packed everything but a damn pair of panties.

Once dressed I stood looking at myself in the mirror. So now I have to avoid pulling a basic instinct move in the office. *I know she did this on purpose.*

I took the elevator up thinking I was going to be able to make it to my desk before anyone really saw me. Great Miguel ass is here bright and early with a small fruit salad for me and I'm guessing a chai latte for him.

"Good morning, Ms. Riggs is there anything you need for me to get started on?" He asked, placing my fruit on my desk and opening the blinds. I liked Miguel, he's a lot to take some time, but he is a breath of fresh air to be around. But this morning I am too distracted to get tangled up in his usual morning foolishness, there is nothing that happens in this office that he does not know about.

"No, can you make sure my morning is clear, I'm a little distracted today and although I think my day is quiet can you please make sure?" I asked, tearing into the fruit salad he brought in.

"Excuse me, Lyne'e can I have a moment, please?" Jamal asked as he leaned against the threshold.

"Sure, Miguel, can you give us a moment? In fact, can you please order breakfast from that restaurant you like? Also prepare my messages, go through the emails from yesterday and get me all messages pertaining to their account." Jamal made sure to close the door behind my nosy Miguel. I watched as Jamal took a seat in the chair across mine before I walked over and stood in front of him. He placed his hands between my thighs and slid his hands until he found the warmest and wettest spot he could and he stroked. He did it so casually as if we were back in his hotel room and not in my office, he didn't stop until he felt me sliding down his fingertips. As he licked his finger, he looked in my eyes. Never said a word, he got up and walked out. I could feel my head spinning again, there is no way I'm going to get a single thing completed today with him in this building.

I was unfocused the entire day. I had blank stares in meetings and slept at my desk for lunch. Jamal was in my head and he knew it. While in a meeting going over the last details for his company's deal, a meeting I really should have been more than alert for, he texted me.

... "I would have never guessed you for the no panty type. I must say I like it. J "1:13 pm

... "well I'm not, it was a one-time incident today. Lynee" 1:15 pm

..."from now on while I'm here, I don't want to see or feel any panties. I like not having to work for it." J 1:16

... "And if I forget to wear them what's in it for me" Lynee 1:20 pm

... "Me. All of me. That's what's in it for you." J 1:21 pm

... "but I've already had you, all of you" Lynee 1:22 pm

... "No baby, I have more to give you. TRUST ME" J 1:23 pm

... " :) " Lynee 1:24 pm

... "lol, you sure this is what you want?" J 1:26 pm

... "I've never been more sure" Lynee 1:28 pm

... "excuse yourself, come back in 3 mins" J 1:30 pm

I did exactly as I was told; I went down the hall to the kitchen nook and poured myself a cup of coffee. When I walked back into the meeting Jamal was sitting in the seat next to mine.. He turned his chair towards mine and scooted closer pretending to show me some reports on his laptop. Again without warning he covertly placed his hands between my legs and for the next hour of the meeting he played with my most sensitive spot. Every time I felt my body getting ready to explode he would stop. I was so angry I wanted to scream, but I knew he'd find some way to take pleasure in it and make me regret even that. Once the meeting was over, we stayed seated, keeping up pointless chatter until the room was empty.

"Go straight to your office" He demanded, standing up and facing me so that I could see the imprint of his aroused manhood. Again I did as I was told and walked as swiftly as I could down the hall with my cell phone to my ear to avoid anyone attempting to spark a conversation with me. Two minutes later, Jamal knocked at my door, turned the lock as he entered and placed me on my desk. I pulled his belt loose as he pulled a condom from his pocket and forced it on. I was too excited to care that this was my work office, there was a growing burning inside of me that only he could control, the moment he was inside of me I wanted to scream. "Be quiet baby" he urged as he placed himself deeper and deeper inside of me. I tried to hide my face in his neck in an effort to muffle the noises that I couldn't control. "*FUCK*" he growled as he gripped my waist tighter, I could feel him shaking uncontrollably and him breathing heavily on my shoulder.

I looked around my office and then at this man standing before me trying to pull himself together. In twenty-six years I had never felt this type of uncontrolled passion. I have never in my life let myself go to be this free, ever. I suddenly became aware that I was at work and found myself wondering if there were camera's or if anyone heard us. Reality wanted to creep in, but my body would not stand for it. Jamal's eye landed on mine and all sense of reality was gone. I could actually feel my body still thriving and this man was no longer even touching me. He watched with this look in his eyes; he looked proud; he watched me unable to control what was coming out of my body he rejoiced, smiled and dropped on his knees.

Before he could even touch me I could feel him breathing on me and it only made me cum harder. His tongue lightly touched my inner thigh, and I moaned, loud enough to force him to place his fingers in my mouth to try to shut me up. This moment wasn't just about him, this was years of me always only doing the right thing and denying myself simple pleasures. This was countless sexual experiences that in comparison I shouldn't even be able to call "sex", this was finally me having a man who would stop at nothing to please me, unfortunately this was all happening on my desk... *at work*. When my body finally calmed down and joined the rest of us on earth, I made the best effort I could to stand, I walked back over to my chair.

"Get your stuff, meet me in the parking lot. I'm not done yet," He demanded as he opened my office door.

"Wait, wait, I can't go anywhere. I physically can't go anywhere." I tried to explain to him.

"Hey Miguel, I don't think Ms. Riggs is feeling well, can you come in here?" he asked.

Miguel walked in slowly looking at us both before giving me the side eye of life. "I'll close things down today, you go home and get some fluids." He suggested in a very salacious tone.

"I'll take her home."

I watched as these two talked amongst themselves like I wasn't even in the room. Miguel walked us to the elevator with a smirk on his face the entire way *he must have heard us.*

Jamal and I went back to his hotel where he used different unknown methods to continuously bring me to orgasmic pleasure until checkout the next morning.

His Side... The Reality

I won't lie, after Lyne'e didn't show up to the house I was pissed. I bought a fucking house for her and she couldn't pull herself away from that wack ass fuckboy long enough to even call and tell me she wasn't coming. I've spent the last couple of weeks in this house, making little repairs, painting, trying to make this place feel like home, but to be completely honest, nothing I do seems to work. Every day, I come here, it's cold, it's quiet, it's empty, it's lonely, it's nothing like the home I wanted.

Work was just the same, yeah I have the big house, yeah I drive the fancy car, I wear the best shit, but I wasn't feeling any of it. At my age I should be hanging with my boys, fuckin' hoes and stumbling into work smelling like pussy, Polo and Henny, not this depressing ass shit. I've grown in this company in half the time that I expected, but it came with strings. The original plan was to head up boardrooms by twenty-five, and have everyone wondering "how do I do it?". When what I really have are long ass meetings with unappreciative clients, who think I'm either too dark or too young to handle their money. And when I'm not explaining my education and experience, I am making up stories trying to hide the fact that Irwin and all the leads under him can't be bothered to attend anything because they're all too busy or too ancient to see the future of investments and finance. But the worst is knowing that the one bitch in the company that I hate the most is fucking her way into my job and my future.

I met a few of my boys at Bomb Pops, one of the hottest strip clubs in Chicago because of its celebrity clientele. On any giving night you can see NBA, NFL and the occasional Oscar winners and nominees. We had a table in the back, celebrating Richie (Richboy) Talan's birthday. Richie was another classmate that we hadn't seen in about a year. He moved to Atlanta after graduation with his longtime girlfriend. The two married straight after college and divorced less than two years later. The upside to Lyne'e not being around is I had more time to kick it with my boys. In between trying to find a new life and work, it's always cool to hang out and laugh at absolutely nothing for once.

The moment I walked through the bar, the smell of cigars and good food instantly assailed me. Our spot was usually the V.I.P. area in the back on a little stage, but I took my time surveying the room for something nice to leave with later on. The place is enormous and the girls are all bad as fuck. If you have a type, you can find at least three of them here, if you have a kink, you can find that here too. If you just like the attention and feel of a woman, this is the best place to spend your time and money in the city. I think that's my favorite part, I can come here, sip my Henny, hit a good cigar, grab me some bomb ass lamb chops and know I'm fucking some bad bitch at the end of the night. Even the women that hang out here look like they belong on stage. Every once in a while Vlad, the guy who owns the joint will host a contest to include the chicks that came to watch. He offered a free bottle to the baddest bitch which was the perfect way to give the girls who were too embarrassed to strip the chance they've always wanted. They throw some ass, the nigga's throw some cash, his girls get a break, the bar makes some money because the girls need liquid courage and all he had to do was give out a free watered down bottle. He keeps me and my boys an open table and I toss him some free financial advice here and there. Win/Win.

On my way to the back I threw a smile to Nikki D, my favorite bartender. She always makes sure my food and drinks are good plus she has the prettiest set of titties I've ever seen. She's never danced here for real, but I have seen her get on the bar a few times if she's had a few. I'd never tell any of my boys because they all press her, but I've hit once or twice since coming here and the shit is amazing.

Nikki D is a wild girl, takes the dick like you wouldn't believe and she likes to spit, suck and swallow. In that order. I was used to college girls; they knew the basics, you may get one to cuff your balls, kiss on her girl or something, but that was the extent of their nasty side. The night Nikki D took me back to her place she fucked my head up. She sat me on her couch, did a little strip show, showing me the few little dances she learned from the club. Sat in my lap, twirled her hair around in my face while grinding hard and slow on my dick. Before she spun around and pulled my legs apart at the knees and unbuckled my belt and then pants. She kept her eyes on mine while she pulled my mans from my boxers and hit it on her lips before running her tongue around the head. Her eyes left mine for a moment, but that was to pull me all the way out of my boxers before, from there she used her mouth to stretch me out, show me her lack of gag reflex and how good she was at not using her hands. She spent the next two songs slowly sucking my dick to the brink of release and she'd let me go. She'd get me there again and she'd let me go. When she was finally tired of playing with me, she spit a mouth full on the head and began jacking me off long enough to catch my release on her on a pair of the prettiest titties I've laid my eyes on. I swear when she finished I was on the corner of her couch in the fetal position.

I walked into her place thinking the hoes from campus were basic; I left her shit realizing I was the lame one. When she finished she wiped herself down, made me a drink before going to take a shower. I thought the night was over, and I was good with that. I would have loved to hit, I'm sure if the pussy was half as good as the mouth I would have torn that shit up, but if she's done than so was I. I didn't want to just leave without saying anything to her, she was mad cool and didn't deserve for me to play her like that. While I waited for her to get out of the shower, I looked at the millions of pictures that she had scattered around her place.

She had pictures with almost everybody in my playlist. I made myself a drink and relaxed as I listened to her belt out vocals I would have never imagined she had. The girl could sing her ass off. Not only was Nikki D pretty, but she could sing, kept a real cool place and knew how to make a nigga feel good. When she finally walked back up front, her fire engine red hair was not black and pulled loosely in a ponytail and her face was shiny and make up free. She wasn't just a pretty girl; she was a beautiful woman. Nikki D has cute dimples and pouty peach lips, she's naturally pretty and quite frankly looked way better without the makeup and hair. We sat on the couch and talked for a while about random shit for almost an hour. I was enjoying her company so much it didn't even occur to me to check my phone or the time.

Just when I was about to tell her it was time for me to go she walked over to me, still in her robe, straddled me, threw her perfect titties in my face and forced one in my mouth. Twenty minutes later she was riding my dick so hard from the back, flinging her hair in my face as she whirled her waist and threw her shoulders back on me add her hands overhead to grab the back of mine. She had me positioned right where she wanted me in front of a mirror in her living room. We both watched her in the mirror as she rode me like her life depended on it.

At first it was clear it was all for show, but when she found her spot, her calculated moves skipped a beat; I grabbed her by her waist and did my best to hold her down while she drove, before we knew it she was cuming and squirming on my dick completely unaware that I had finished already. I don't know when it happened, but when I woke up I was laying flat on my back on the carpet with one hand on my dick and the other hand reaching out for God. The next day I realized I wasn't really ready to settle down and get married. I knew I was missing something out here.

She and I fucked like that a few more times, each time nastier than the one before. Each time in that living room on that couch then or on the floor. The issue with Nikki D is she's too much for me. The more we fucked around the more she felt comfortable and her inner freak really like to come out. I'm willing to try almost anything but I wasn't really ready for the shit she's into. She once pulled out her toy box like it was a normal thing. I looked inside while she continued to take a mouth full of me in, slowly dragging me in and out of her mouth, but never taking her eyes off me. She had me so distracted I didn't know what to focus on, her or the various pink, purple or clear vibrators in the box. She had one in damn near every color of the rainbow and no two were alike.

Before I could utter a single word and ask her why she brought the box out she was sliding some ring on my dick.

Every time I fucked with Nikki D she had me feeling like a lame, the shit she was into was nothing like the shit I had seen or done. The ring had its own dildo attached to it. She covered it with lube then placed the bottle in my hand before asking me if I was ready. The only question on my mind was ready for what? Shit, I won't front, initially I was a little intimidated, but not as much as I was a little offended. I'd been giving her my best shit all that week then she goes and pulls out a fucking dick too attached to my real thing. I didn't know what to think; I didn't know what to do; I didn't really understand what was supposed to go where, but then she took her sweet time coaching me through just how she liked it. The level of debauchery and perversion that I partook in that night still blows my mind.

The entire drive home all I could think about was the ideal of her easing me into her kink. If that was her way of slow walking me into her reality, I knew I was out of my league. Plus, she likes it a little rougher than I'm used to. I never know what line I'm crossing with her that shit scares me. After the time I spent with Nikki D, I knew not only was I not ready to be married, but I didn't know half the shit I thought I did.

When I finally made it through the sea of cigar smoke and glitter, I made it to the table with some of the crew. Our circle is small but effective. Da'vere and I aren't from here, we met all of these cats through our jobs, my cousin Brian and Da'vere's building. At the table was Da'vere, Mike H., Mike D., and Javari. I work with Mike H., he introduced us to his boy Mike D., and Javari worked with Da'vere. Rich grew up in Brian's neighborhood. We used to hoop together when my family came to visit as kids and when I moved here; we linked back up. Everyone made their own money and everyone was doing their own thing. We were a group of successful young black men, there wasn't a stereotype amongst us. Everyone had credit, cars and a castle of some sort to lay their heads, if you didn't like us it was obvious why, you wanted to be one of us. We all had our own reason for needing a night out. The problem with always having it together is no one wanted to admit when they didn't, but we can always rely on Da'vere to highlight the obvious.

Da'vere is my closest friend but by far was the worst type of man. He could never date my sisters and if my future unborn daughters were to ever come home, with a man like him I could easily see myself behind bars. When Lyne'e and I agreed to move to Chicago he came with us. Da'vere was a country boy, grew up in Louisiana with his dad, Dr. Emery Young. His mom and dad never married, but his dad had full custody. Da'vere's mom wasn't dead or even a deadbeat, she just wasn't equipped to go against Dr. Young. She had one affair compared to Dr. Young's dozen, and he left her. Dr. Young was nothing to play with, in fact he is down right fucking mean as shit. Like a lot of mean men I knew he was a smart one, calculated and manipulative. He knew the best way to hurt Da'vere's mom, and that was to take Da'vere from her. The few times I've met the guy, he was riding Da'vere about not being a doctor, the way he dressed, the way he walked, shit I remember him calling him out for the way he breathed. He was supposed to finish school and come back home to help grow the family clinic. Ultimately Da'vere's decision to move to Illinois meant he was cut off.

Thankfully, his grandparents stepped in and helped him out. Much like Dr. Young, grandpa Young was spiteful and knew the best way to hurt his son was through Da'vere as well. The man came from generational fuck up-ness. The way he explained it to me after his dad refused to pay for last-minute graduation stuff was, his dad had always been an asshole and spread his bitterness around. He didn't just keep Da'vere from his mom; he kept him from everyone. Da'vere's grandparents paid his rent, leased him a car and even helped him with a job here as soon as his feet touched Illinois soil. By the time Da'vere was twenty-six he was a pharmacist studying for his PhD and easily out earned all of us. Everyone saw the potential he had, everyone but Da'vere. All he thinks about is pussy and money, and in no particular order. He didn't care who he had to lie to or steal from to get either.

He treated women the same way his dad treated them and ultimately his mother. Being raised by a successful black man in the south made him a misogynist. He's been that way for as long as I can remember. The conflict is, he's also the first to fall on his sword or will give you his last if you need it. He's usually the loudest, drunkest person in the room, he wanted all eyes on him regardless of how stupid he looked, sound or act. And tonight was no different. It's Richie's birthday, but Da'vere made sure that every round ass in the club sat in his lap first. I've always hated the attention, damn near every fight I ever got into, Da'vere caused it. He was always trying to holla at somebody's girl and if he had an audience; it was always worse. Most times it worked, there was something about him that women liked. In college he played QB, the little nigga was fast and tactical on and off the field. I think we got along so well because he was so extra all the time, it just made me look that much better. I learned very early that the hoes that's only in it for show or money always wanted the Da'vere's of the crew, but the real baddies, the independent ones, the ones who were proud not to need a nigga for shit other than good dick always fell for the chill and low key nigga by his side. Shit, I never have to do much when he was around. You're going to have a good time, but the problem was he never knew when to chill and that almost always ended with us having to drag him out of a spot.

After the drinks started flowing, so did the conversations. Richie told us how he got caught entertaining a young lady in the back of his truck one night at a bowling alley. He was out with some coworkers and one kept trying to throw him the ass. Things went too far after a drink or two that he should not have had, she stepped outside for a smoke and asked if he would come with her for protection, to which he kindly obliged. They walked around to his truck, ironically parked in the back of the lot and as soon as they turned the corner she went for it. He laughed as he recalled how she pulled his dick out right there and began sucking him. The guys all laughed and gave each other's pounds as Richie continued.

As he was talking he went through his phone and pulled up a picture of the chick Robin and passed it around the table. He explained it wasn't even the first time she had done that. This bowl'n Blow was becoming a regular thing for them. He wanted to back out but John, his all too eager boss insisted he played. They all met every Wednesday after work and every time, by 7:45 pm the two would go outside for a smoke and she would without fail give him head by the side of the truck. She was too good at it, he would see her face when making love to his wife. She would send pictures to him on his work phone, nasty text messages and occasionally' videos. Although he knew it was wrong, Richie loved it. He had never had a female so interested in him; he rationalized it by telling himself he hadn't slept with her so it's not as bad as it looked.

The table was divided, the single guys all agreed it wasn't that bad, while the others knew what it was and told him he should have called them, they would have told him to get out while he could. Richie took his last shot and continued telling us the sorted details of his failed marriage. She knew well that he was married, every time Michelle, his wife would come to the office she would speak and bring her coffee or water. And every time Michelle would leave she would give him a hand job anywhere they could avoid the cameras. She was a young freak and Richie loved it. She did all the things his wife wouldn't do, and she did them without spending his check or nagging him.

Richie continued to tell us how bad it was to see his wife pack up and leave, how he never realized how much she did for them. Sure it felt good to be adored by someone, anyone, but it was all superficial. He didn't know the first thing about Robin and didn't care to. He didn't want her taking care of him when he was sick; he didn't want her walking around his home, and he didn't want her to have his children. She was fun, exciting and had no limits, but she was a risk and his job was to spot risk. He shook his head as he thought about all that he lost taking one risk.

I don't know if it was the alcohol or the sad and honest truth from Rich, but I put my drink down and admitted something I couldn't even admit to myself. Well, not for real.

"I fucked up too" I mumbled. Part of me hoped I was so low that no one heard me, the other part was just glad to get it off of my chest. Yeah, I did my thing in college but when Lyne'e and I moved here to Chicago, I told myself that was it.

"Nigga you didn't" Da'vere questioned, while putting his drink down. "You fucked that shit up with Lyne'e? She don't ask for shit, how they fuck you ruin that?" He questioned. All of this time I thought he couldn't stand her, but the look on his face right now says different, he almost look disappointed in me. "Is that why you've been walking around looking like shit?"

Saying it out loud actually made me feel bad. If I'm being honest with myself I had been doing my thing a lot in the past year. I really tried to keep my shit tight and not fuck with these hoes, but I fucked up. The guys all moved in close and I swear it felt like the music got lower and the lights were brighter, just on me as I began.

"It really isn't much to tell or different from Richie, there was a young lady that I worked with who had little or no concept of the word NO. There was little she objected to and was always willing to out perform her last performance. She even had a roommate that she would offer to bring along." I smiled thinking about the first time shit that happened. At the time I convinced myself I was doing it out of respect for my girl. This chick did all the things I knew Lyne'e wouldn't and I wouldn't dare ask her.

"Full transparency, I am ashamed, but this shit here is supposed to be a judgment free zone so fix your fucking face Richie." I laughed.

"I'm just saying, how the hell did you fuck that up?" He asked, tipping his beer at the fellas.

"The moment I began to make something of myself I traded my black queen for an ivory princess. I had been spending so much of my time working close with them at work it was almost inevitable." I joked. Yet every guy at the table all agreed in some form or fashion. "Yeah, my parents were cool and was real big on love is love, but I was also taught to love, honor and respect my black queen. Sadly, the moment I was in that office, I found myself swimming in a sea of blue and green eyes, all smitten by the theory of the black Mandingo. I felt compelled."

They weren't all white girls, there was the green-eyed Angel. I met her at the bank and pursued her to bring some of her business to our firm. She owned a nail salon in one building downtown and was looking to expand. We talked on the walk back to her car about investments. A few days later she walked her cafe caramel ass into my office and a week after that she had it riding backwards on my dick in the back of her shop. She wasn't polished; she spoke with an east coast accent and she hadn't graduated from high school, but she had street smarts and her hustle was greater than mine. She was self made, owned three salons in the area and was well on her way to having a million dollar empire by the time she was thirty. She carried a gun, fucked with street nigga's, and she didn't make time for bullshit. We met up on her schedule, when she wanted it. She never asked about my girl, she never asked for anything honestly, she paid for her services from the firm and never mentioned a discount or a favor. She was a different beast than I was used to. When she batted those green eyes, I came running. Angel Eye's loved to roll up, fuck and roll up again and when we were done, she'd hop into her jeep and ride out into the sunset. She was the type of bitch you dreamed about, about her money, loved the dick and had no time for small talk. Fact is, after Lyne'e left, I considered going at Angel for real, but I had never been so ignored by a woman like she ignored me. She said something about me not being the type of man that she really wanted; I had a woman at home, but I couldn't keep my dick in my pants. She was right, even when she said it, I couldn't get mad. Granted, she didn't include the facts that I wasn't hugging the block or in local shoot outs twice a week, but I got the point. Besides, she was right; I had a good woman that I couldn't be faithful to, there was no telling what I would do with a woman like her. Plus, with Lyne'e out of the picture I started talking to these females more, and I was just not interested. Angel could hold her own in a conversation, but getting her to make time for a conversation was like pulling teeth. Fitting into her schedule was fine when I didn't have the time, but now that I do, there was no way I was going to wait for a bitch to make time for me.

Lyne'e is my muse, she challenges me; she encourages me; she is my mental and spiritual guidance and now I may lose her being stupid. I don't want to be Richie, sad and lonely. Or like Mr. Young, wealthy and lonely. Spending money on dates and paying bitches to fuck. Or worse, have a woman in my life who's only here for what I can do for her. I want to be with someone I can trust to not try to fuck me out of my money, but someone who really has my back.

Da'vere interrupted me "You two fools are just alike. You both were happier with white women. As beautiful as they are, black women come with too many issues." He proclaimed before finishing his drink.

Everybody threw their hands in the air and laughed. But it didn't stop him from continuing to share his dumbass unsolicited opinion "I've dated and fucked them all, and every time I walk away feeling like shit it was with black women. Their advantage used to be their bodies, but have you seen these new bitches now? These white girls got ass. They're just as thick, they've learned to make macaroni and cheese, cornbread and pork chops just like momma used to make. They come to the table with good credit and now they openly want the dick." Not one of the guys agreed, but some dumbass sitting at the table next to us offered to buy him a drink. *Yeah like this idiot needs another drink.* "I'm just saying nowhere have I seen a sign saying black girls only. You fools keep trying to wife these 'I don't need a man', 'I make as much money as you do', 'bout that life' chicks if you want to. Y'all all gone be lonely with a dry dick and since Richie you don't want the freak that takes dick under work tables please give me her number and I'll have her thanking God for baby Jesus by the end of the night." He laughed.

As much as we all hate Da'vere's vulgar approach to women, we couldn't help but laugh. Mainly because for the rest of the night, not a single woman in that club danced for him. Da'vere had his heart broken by his college love, Jada. She left him for a baseball player named Chad Moore, third-round draft pick for Cleveland, who couldn't keep up and ended up getting benched. Chad left Jada for a wannabe pop star and she came running back to Da'vere. Da'vere took her back only for her to cheat on some lame ass nigga that used to hang around the campus selling to everyone. She ended up flunking out and babymomma number three. Da'vere has been done with black women ever since. It's not even just black women, Da'vere really despised women altogether. The Mike's secretly had bet to see when he would come out of the closet for years.

I drove home with the music as loud as I could get it. If Lyne'e knew about the other woman, she would have flipped out and killed us all. I never gave any of these women the thought or impression that they stood a real chance, so I know none of them reached out to her. I kept my shit tight, so she didn't find any numbers or condoms in our place, so for the life of me I can't figure out why things between us had gotten so bad. We have been together since we were eighteen years old and now she won't even return my calls. That's how you treat a nigga you met in the club, not someone you've invested real time with. She didn't even acknowledge my flowers. That fucking bouquet cost me over a hundred dollars and nothing.

As I pulled in the driveway, I realized it had been over two months since I've seen her last. *Did she really move on, is she really fucking with ol'boy? The corney ass clown with the cheap loafers.*

I wanted to say fuck it. If she thinks she can do better than me, fuck it, she can try. At twenty-six, I have more than most nigga's do at forty. It ain't shit this clown can do for her that I haven't already done. If she does fuck him, she'll just be doing all the shit I've taught her. This muthafukka should be fucking thanking me. *Fuck her.*

Her Side... The Revelation

Bright and early Sunday morning, Keyla and I went for a run. Well really I ran, Keyla just kind of was there in the beginning and at the end. I spent the weekend eating junk and drinking; I needed to purge. We talked about Anderson and Jamal, King Mally Mal as Sloane playfully called him. Fact is Jamal will be leaving soon headed back to Vermont, and I didn't want a relationship, let alone a long distance one, but I did want something. Then there was Anderson, to me he has always been safe, my ideal of a home, my great love. Before now, I realize he were those things because he was all I had ever really known. I can't compare highschool boyfriends to real grown up shit. Hell, you even have to be seventeen to watch any good movies. My entire scope of real love is focused around Anderson, so its only right that I thought he was the moon and stars.

Then in walk this man who has knocked my entire world out of orbit and I like it. But I can't compare a few amazing nights, *hmmm days and weekends too* to years of friendship and commitment. I can say for certain now that I've had something different, something amazing, I felt the playing field was a little more even. I could never say for sure that Anderson has fucked around since we moved to Chicago, but I know he was doing something. All of the late nights with the boy's, the random days missing at work in meetings. I could always tell, just like when we would get into it at college, he had tells, even if he thinks that I didn't know.

All of that aside, the question would remain, could I go back to the mediocre and safe after being with Jamal. *What if he came back to town, could I tell him no, would I even want to tell him no? What if Jamal didn't want to leave me alone, what if he wanted to stay and be with me? What if he wanted me to move to Vermont with him? Do black people even live in Vermont? Could I give up everything, was I ready to give up Anderson? After all, he had been my constant for years; I loved him. Yes, this past year has been rough, but that's one year.* We have been together for almost eight years, we've spent our party years wrapped up in each other and trying to take off professionally at that.

We had a life plan, a plan that he threw out the window whenever he found it convenient, a plan that he put his career ahead of, even our union. The focal point of our life plan was our marriage, shit he didn't even really propose, he just told me we were going to marry after we got "settled" in Chicago and I went along. His career will always come first, that's clear. I can't spend my life being second to a career, that means he will never take mine seriously and what about a family. The family he swore he wanted and that he talked me into.

I ran faster.

The possibility of four children, the birth of those children, family trips, holidays everything would be an afterthought to his job. That was not the man or life that I wanted. I want a man like my father, someone who knew the value of a dollar but knew the value of family was way higher. But now I also want a man to make me feel like Jamal did, this man came in like a fucking wrecking ball. Tearing down boundaries and my wall, *Lord, yes, my walls* with no concern for anything else. Someone willing to work hard at life and at love, not just a man who knows how to earn a buck or two. Shit, I can earn a good income, but I don't want to have children just to let a nanny raise them or to complete an ideal or image.

Before I knew it, I was back at home sitting on the floor by the bathroom, waiting for Sloane to get out of the shower.

"You look like you had a good run, you feeling okay?" She questioned, walking past me to her bedroom.

"Yeah, I just needed to think."

"And how did that work out for you?"

"It didn't."

"Let me help you." Sloane offered, peeking her wet head out of her bedroom door. "Keep Jamal."

"Of course you would say that you hate Anderson and he and I have so much history." I pointed out.

"Keep Jamal."

"But Anderson and I have been through so much."

"And I'm sure that if you give him the chance he'll put you through even more. Jamal is a great guy and more importantly, he's a great guy that seems to really be into you. Anderson had his chance, and he blew it." She argued before readjusting her towel. Besides, he only popped up the other night because his dick senses tingled, he knew you were getting ready to let that thang out, and as usual his ass was hating." She scuffed.

After a long hot shower Sloane and I decided to do some retail therapy. We grabbed Keyla on our way to the city to just have a day. I didn't come from a big family, my sister and I have always been from two different planets, I don't have a gang of cousins that I hang out with, it's always just been me. Maybe me and a few girls from school, but for the most part it's been just me, so on those days that I can get together with my girls and do anything it's always a great time. Keyla life is so complicated most of the time. There's either twenty people living with her or her man at the time, so our time is always limited. Sloane and I may live together, but we really do not get to spend as much time together as I like, and nothing made me feel more like a boss than riding around in her new all black Range Rover stuffed with shopping bags. We took a break from shopping to grab lunch, Mani and Pedi's then to catch a movie. It was exactly the type of day that I needed, and judging by the vibration in my phone I may get to end it with great dick too!

"Where you at, I want to see you?" J 6:57 pm

"Out with the girls, leaving the movies. I'm actually downtown now" Lynee 6:59 pm

"Cool, how about I take you ladies out for a drink" J 7:01

"Sounds like a plan meet us on Michigan Ave at Pirriza's" Lynee 7:05 pm

I stared out of the window thinking about Jamal and how much fun he has been. This man blew into my life like a damn breeze and has completely changed my way of life.

"Look at you, smiling ear to ear." Sloane laughed.

"Shut up, you don't even know what I'm smiling at."

"Yes I do, the woman in that car over there knows what you're smiling at." Sloane teased.

"So let me make sure I have this and I will never bring it back up again." Keyla asked. "You have met this guy, who checks all of your crazy over the top boxes. He has a career, kid free, life-changing dick and you're going to give that up for Anderson? The same Anderson that you have been fucking for years, who in the last seven years may have actually giving you seven orgasm, while King Mal has giving you seven in one day and you are going to give that up?"

"You do know sex is not everything right?" I asked, checking my lip gloss in the side mirror.

"Says who?" Both Sloane and Keyla replied in unison.

"It's not everything but it does say a lot. Look at it like this, a good lover is attentive, patient, and giving. Three things that also make a good man. Three things we all know Anderson is not. That man only cares about himself, always has. I'm just saying, if he was half as good as he thinks he is, Jamal wouldn't have stood a chance with you. Me yes, but not you." Keyla laughed. "You're a good girl, loyal, crazy, but loyal. You found the pot of gold at the end of the rainbow and the big dick leprechaun protecting it. Do you really want to let that go, for Anderson?"

The rest of the ride was quiet. Truthfully I had no rebuttal for what either of these two had to say. Before we got out of the truck, I asked the girls one last time. "What if he's not worth it, what if I give everything up and I lose in the end?"

Sloane smiled at me and brushed my hair out of my face. "Girl, you let that man play with that thang at work, bend you over at your desk and eat it in the parking garage on a sunny Thursday afternoon. You. If that's not worth it, then what would you do for someone that is?"

I wanted to hit her as she and Keyla burst out laughing. "I mean come on babe, sex ain't everything, we all know and agree, but this isn't just about sex. You've opened up in a way that you never have, for someone that you don't even know. Meanwhile, this clown you've spent forever with can't get over himself long enough to really make you happy. Smart money is on the man who is man enough to talk yo ass out of your panties and walk around with them in his pocket. Shit, you only live once and what a way to do it." Keyla added.

When we walked into the restaurant Jamal was already sitting at the bar with four shots in front of him. The girls were nice enough to let our first drink settle in before they began grilling him. He and Sloane have met a few times in the past couple of weeks, but this was Keyla's first crack at him. I watched as he laughed and squirmed at her crazy antics and blushed at some of her more uncomfortable questions. Typically, I would have objected, but she asked all the questions that until now I was too stupid to ask.

Things like did he see a future with me, how would things work with him in Vermont and me here in Chicago? Is he looking for a relationship or just something to do in town, could he see himself moving here to be with me? What did his brother look like? When her line of questions stopped Sloane's started, we were thirty questions into our evening before they let the man come up for air.

Jamal was a gentleman if nothing else, where most men would not have been bothered or irritated with my dear nosy friends he smiled and indulged them.

"I am willing to do whatever Lyne'e feels comfortable with. Personally I think her heart is somewhere else and although I genuinely enjoyed every second that I am able to spend with her over the last couple of days I can't say what our future looks like." His brown eyes slowly drifted over to mine as he licked his lips and continued "Trust me, this woman is amazing and if she said the word, I would pack it up and move here tomorrow, but I know when to bow out. She's torn somewhere else, I think she's a bit of a masochist and the ideal of a new healthy one is scary for her, so I'm going to fall back and let her sort her thoughts and feelings out. I'm aware all good things must come to an end."

I don't know what it was about this man but he sees me. *A little too well.* If I could draw up a perfect man Jamal would be him, he was handsome as hell, attentive, sexy, educated, yet still just hood enough and could fuck me to some orgasmic center of the universe. But he was not Anderson. I smiled and looked deeply in his eyes, blushing I'm sure as I felt his hands caress my thigh. Sloane thanked Jamal for their drinks and slice before she and Keyla excused themselves for the evening. Jamal paid the bill and then we left. This last night was everything, he dominated me in a way I never thought I could like. I had always heard about this type of experience, but always turned my nose up to it. *There is no way I'd ever let a man control me.* What the fuck was I thinking, that man made me his puppet, working me inside and out. Our bodies melted together and formed a new solid and then melted again. One last time I was a slave to his debauchery, I fucking loved every second of it. My orgasms were no longer mine, they were trophies that he took pride in. We didn't sleep that night; we didn't do much talking; we studied each other's bodies from the crown of our heads to the padding on our feet, and when the morning came, we were done. Jamal left his mark on me and I had the bites and scars to prove it.

Later that week, there was a knock at my office door. Before I could complete the phrase "come in" I could see a burst of color and Miguel's shiny Prada loafers walking through the door. "Somebody has been a good-bad girl, an arrangement like this had to have cost a fortune" Miguel chimed as he picked through the flowers looking for the card.

"Oh so you're saying you didn't get me flowers for not killing you when you spilled hot coffee on my favorite cream pea coat." I sarcastically replied as I snatched the card from his hands.

"Thinking about you, missing you, NEED YOU."

"Yeah, you have been a very bad girl, nobody smiles like that for no reason". Miguel gushed as he walked out the door. I knew who the flowers were from the moment I read the card. We agreed to cut it all off cold turkey, but I must admit I've been thinking real hard about taking him up on the flight he promised me. Shit, I've been thinking real hard about walking there if I had to. The way that man moved his body was not natural. He had cleverly broken our "let it rest" agreement. And that's what I like about him, how he knew what I needed before I knew made our time together even more amazing.

Lost in recent memories I didn't even notice the knock at my door. Still with the card in my hand and a very familiar moisture creeping in out of my body, I was surprised to see Anderson standing there with a much smaller, less colorful arrangement of flowers in his hand. The moment our eyes met, it was like someone let all the air out of the room. If this was a cartoon, his jaw would have hit the flower and his flowers would have fallen over limp and died.

"Anderson, hi, what are you doing here?" I stammered over the words. "I mean how are you? I'm surprised to see you." My words started to come together as I slowly slid the card under some paper on my desk.

"I'm too late, I see." he said, shocking himself with his own sincerity.

"Come in, close the door and sit down please" I asked as I moved Jamal's flowers to the side of my desk. I wanted to lie and say they were from a client, but why, I didn't owe him an explanation. "So how are you, how have things been? I asked.

"Clearly not as good as things have been for you. Your office is nice, you're smiling and the flowers. Remind me to give these to your assistant on my way out. I'm sure he'll appreciate them." He added swinging the flowers around.

"No, they're beautiful. Thank you!" I replied walking over to take the bouquet from him. "So what brings you here?"

"Honestly, I don't know. I wanted to see you, I missed you, but I get it now. This is why you haven't been returning my calls."

Anderson has always been great at earnest honesty, he has no problem telling you how he feels and I do love that about him. I couldn't help but chuckle at the "returning his calls" part, I can only think of three, maybe four missed calls from him. "Can I be honest with you?" I asked, walking back around to my chair. "I haven't returned your calls because I don't know what to say. I feel like we loved each other because it's what we feel we are supposed to do, but I don't really think that it is genuine anymore. I mean, I've always loved you, whole heart in, but I've had time to think about it, and I don't think you've really loved me the same."

"How can you say that, so you only loved me because you felt obligated to?" He asked in his angry work voice.

"No, I'm not saying that. I'm saying we began wanting different things, you found the career you wanted and quickly left me behind. You weren't treating me like someone you loved, more like I was the obligation or only here as a source of emotional support. You really didn't appreciate me or view me as a partner. Anderson you didn't even touch me like I was your soon to be wife. We had sex like robots. Like we were playing a game, and you only did the moves to get to the end of the board. Pleasing me was an optional board, but you used a cheat code to get around it."

"Oh, so now you fucking some random nigga and all of a sudden I wasn't hitting it right?" He blurted out angrily. "I'm almost glad you fucking that wack ass nigga, I sure you showed him all the shit I taught you. Ha, you're fucking hilarious, suddenly after all of these years I don't know how to fuck? Trust me you're the only one complaining."

It was with that comment that I suddenly realized how much I loved my freedom, and my girl Tisha popped in my head. Tisha has been doing my hair since I was a teenager. I don't know what I would do if I couldn't go sit in her chair and have my scalp massaged. *I'm sure I can't get that type of treatment in prison.*

For a moment I stood there silent, frozen and caught off guard by the proclamation that this man just made to me. *I'm the only one complaining. Hmmmmm.* For a very brief second I entertained the ideal of telling him how amazingly I had been fucked, right there in that seat he was currently perched in. I really want to tell his ass that in less than a month a man had turned me on my head and all the way the fuck out, when he had me for years and could barely make me cum. As I look at him sitting on the edge of his seat thinking that his "only one complaining" comment had really broke me I decided the best move was to move the fuck on. I had never been more sure that Anderson was weak as fuck as I did in the very moment.

I laughed "I said all of that and all you heard was about sex? I hope them hoes you fucking keep giving you 10's across the board! I hope with all of my little heart they don't ever complain about it. I hope when you roll over on your back out of breath and catch a charlie horse that you keep on thinking it's because you just put it down." I laughed thinking about the last time we had sex and I had to go take a shower to finish the job he couldn't. I shook it off and continued. "It's just like you to only hear sex in everything that I said, because that's who you are, a man who only knows how to have sex. A selfish little man with no heart, no love, not a care in the fucking world for anyone other than you and yo dick. Anderson, you didn't make time for me. Do you know how many nights I ate dinner alone? Or how many times I had to catch a cab or a ride home because you just couldn't be bothered? What about all the times you accuse me of doing something stupid like leaving the lights on or dishes around the house, by passing the fact that you leave your clothes everywhere? Do you know how many arguments we had that could have been avoided with you simply saying 'my bad, I meant to say'? Do you know how many times I just wanted you to notice that I exist and you ignored anything that I had an interest in. And you think this is just about sex? I mean, I always figured you were having sex with someone, but I just never really wanted to press you to find out. You spent more time feeding your ego than you did feeding us. You were the one who treated our relationship like an obligation, I just couldn't continue taking it anymore."

I tried with all of my might not to shed a tear in front of him. "Anderson, you didn't even propose to me, you told me we would be married, and I foolishly went along with it. I can't spend my life being in your background, like I'm some fucking accessory to the Great Anderson Hobbs life. If you don't value me or even want to be with me, you could have left a long time ago, I honestly don't even know why you are here now."

I sat across from Anderson fuming; I swear I could feel actual heat radiating from my body and this large ball of emotion crawling up my stomach, chest and now throat. I wanted to look away; I wanted to do anything else, but what my body was preparing to do. At this point I had absolutely no control, I was too angry and hurt. I couldn't stop the tears from filling my eyes if I tried. My only hope now, is to not have an ugly cry coupled with loud sobs. The last thing I need is for my coworkers to hear me crying in my office and Anderson walk out. I waited for a response, a mumble, a stutter from him but he just sat there. "I was devastated when I left, and you barely reached out to me. You texted me and asked if I was good. Like I tripped and fell or like I took too long to come home. You called me four times, Anderson. Four times, we shared an entire home and when you came home to see that I had left, you shot me a fucking text message. That was how much you cared about me, about us. No, I didn't want you to chase me, but you could have at least pretending to care. Then you pop up one night, uninvited, ruin my evening, square up with my date as if either one of us owed you something, and all is supposed to be forgiving? You didn't fight for us, you didn't give a fuck, all you care about is you and that was the reason I left."

"You left because you weren't getting your way?" Anderson snapped.

"No, I left because you often came home smelling like perfume, weed or worse. I left because I was tired of lying to myself about where you were or who you were with. I left because you didn't have time for me or for us. I left because you spent more time doing you, than you did doing me and when you did it was half ass. I left because you let your precious Irwin overlook and take advantage of me and my intelligence, even worse Anderson you took advantage of me and my intelligence. Anderson I left because you are selfish as fuck and don't know how to love anyone other than yourself. But we can say you're right, I wasn't getting my way."

His Side ... The Self Discovery

I sat in that office and listened as Lyne'e basically called me a bum ass nigga. I wanted to cut her off, defend what was left of my good name, but I knew that would prove her exactly right. Instead I sat silently in an internal apoplectic manner and listened as she made me out to be a fucking monster, who treated her like shit and never valued her. The only reason she was making what she did at that damn company is because of me. No one walks into that company earning what she was earning unless you were family or fucking. I put her on my team. Since the day I laid eyes on her I have never treated another bitch the way I treated her. Now she's attacking me as a man and I just can't be okay with this.

This shit she's crying about just proves my point, she wanted me to chase her. This was never about anything other than she was in her feelings, couldn't keep up and wanted me to run after her like we were in a muthafucking movie. I mean some of the shit she has to say is right; I know I could have done things differently, but she wasn't hurting for a damn thing. I didn't miss a birthday, Valentine's Day, Christmas or any of her made up holidays. I wanted to tell her that I could change, that I would change, but I couldn't get the words to actually come out. Even if I did, they would be a lie. All of this shit is not on me.

"You know what, maybe you are too late." She snapped, wiping the tears from her eyes. "I wish I could tell you that I moved on and that someone else was doing all of the things that you weren't but the truth of the matter is, that's not even the case. I've changed on my own. I've outgrown the ride or die bitch you wanted me to be. I have no intention of settling for you or anyone else ever again. If I can't be someone's everything, then I'd rather be alone. I'm finding out who I am and I like her. I've been with you for years Anderson and honestly I don't see the point anymore. I'm smart, I make good money, I have a good head on my shoulders all because I work hard. I may not be everybody's type, but I'm pretty and I have a good heart. These may not be things that you value, but they are some of the things that I do and I know a real man will. I've let you treat me like shit for too long, babe I'm over it, so yes you are too late."

Fuck. Of all the ways I saw this playing out, I was never expecting it to play out like this. I appreciated her, but I guess she needed more, and now it's too late, so what's the point of interrupting her?

"I fucked up, I see that now. For what it's worth I'm sorry. I wish you would have told me how you felt at the time. I wish I would have known so that I could have given you what you needed. I really wish you would have been real with me, I would have fixed it, before you found yourself hating me. Before we got this far. I hate that you let me think that we were good and growing when you clearly didn't feel the same. Rather you believe it or not, there's nothing I wouldn't have done to fix us or to make us right, had you just talked to me." I wanted to say more, but if I'm honest with myself, there's no point?

I smiled at my beautiful ex as I walked out of her office. I felt defeated. If there was something else that I could do, I have no idea what it was. As I stepped off the elevator, I pulled my phone out and called the one person who has always been a constant in my life and who will always be direct and honest with me.

"Hi momma, how are you doing"

"I'm good baby, how are you doing?" Just the sound of her warm voice made me feel comforted.

"Momma I've been better. I messed up, and I messed up bad." I confessed.

"Still no Lyne'e huh?"

"No, I tried. I really did, but I think it's officially over."

"Tell me baby, what did you try?" I could hear the condescending tone in her voice, she was ready to pounce. I would try to back out of the conversation but again, that would just be proving Lyne'e's point. "I'm sure you two can work through this. That's a great girl, I know your not stupid enough to let her get away."

"I bought this house, you know, for us and she won't even take my calls. Today I went by her job and she basically said 'I'm not shh'.." I stuttered hoping that she didn't hear my slip up, "Clearly she's dating someone, she has flowers at her desk. She's done, she basically said she was done with me."

"But why, tell me what did you do to get you two to this point?" I knew the answer, I knew of a few answers, but I dare not tell my momma all of them.

"I wasn't there for her how she felt I should have been. Momma, Lyne'e has always been so independent, I didn't even realize that I wasn't giving her the attention she needed. She never said anything, before I knew it, she quit her job and started another one without even asking me. We are supposed to be a team, we walked into that company together and she just got up and quit like that." Just thinking about it pissed me off all over again.

"Anderson, who do you think you are? I know I'm no Mother Mary, so you damn sure ain't no young Jesus. Who the hell are you to demand that she ask your permission? Is that what this is about, you think she needs your permission to make a decision about her life?"

"What? momma no, that's not what I said." I scoffed.

"Yes, it was. Then you say you two were a team, were you a team when you moved up the food chain and left her behind? Were you two a team when you postponed y'all wedding without even talking to her about it? Were you two a team when she did tell you her plans for a new job?" I wanted to ask how she knew all of that, but I knew better than to interrupt. "It's mighty funny how you only know how to be on a team when it benefits you. That is not the man I raised, to be selfish and arrogant. That young lady gave you more time than I would have and she deserved better than an egotistical megalomaniac trying to keep her under his thumb." I just listened. There was nothing I could say, for the second time today.

I pulled up to my house ten minutes ago, but I'd dare not cut momma off.

"Anderson, you fix things with that girl before it's really too late."

"But momma, I'm telling you it's too late. She's been seeing some guy and today, today was a disaster. I haven't seen her cry in so long, but today, she could barely get her words out past the crying. At one point she didn't even yell. She just looked me in my eyes and said it was too late. At least if she yelled I could have a chance to comfort her or apologize and ask to make it up."

"Anderson, we talked to Lyne'e three days ago. She called to wish your dad a happy birthday. If it was over, do you think she would still be calling us? Think." Momma demanded.

She called my dad? Shit, I forgot to call my own dad, but Lyne'e remembered. "Okay, I'll give her a call tomorrow when she has calmed down."

"You will call her tonight, while she's hurting. Waiting for her to calm down only helps you. You're too scared to accept your punishment, but you have no problem passing out pain and hurt to others. You hurt her, asking for forgiveness is never easy, but doing what's right hardly ever is, and I know we taught you that. Now stop being a coward and call her, help her heal so that you two can grow and I can get my grandbabies." Momma laughed.

I couldn't do anything but laugh and agree, "I love you, woman."

"I love you too baby" she replied before hanging up the phone.

I knew my momma was right, but it was the last thing that I wanted to hear. I was hoping for her to see things my way, but she didn't even let me explain *my way*. After sitting in front of my house for another ten minutes, I turned off my engine. I was on my way inside when my phone rang, it was my homeboy Chris. Thank goodness, he always has some mess going on and right now I could use the distraction.

"What up?"

"Yo, you in the house for the night?" Chris asked frantically.

"Nah, I'm actually just about to walk in the door. Why, what's up?"

"Dude I fucked up, bad. Meet me at the bar?" Chris asked before ending the call.

I pressed play on my car radio and drove slowly downtown. I can't imagine what Chris could have gotten himself into, but I hope this fool doesn't ask to borrow some money. I pulled up to the bar, tipped the valet to leave my car up front and walked in like I owned the place. Bang was our favorite after work hangout. Every fine thick ass broad with a job came through here at least once a week. I don't know if it's the heavy poured drinks, the delicious mouth watering food or the banging Dj, but when you need to unwind after a long workday or just looking for some company for the night Bang was the spot to chill at.

I spotted Chris sitting up front at the edge of the bar with two empty glasses in front of him. He was in jeans, a polo shirt and gym shoes, so clearly he wasn't coming from work. He was hunched over and working on drink number three when I approached him. As he turned to speak I noticed his eyes were red, as if he had been crying and his lip was split. He didn't even look at me, he tossed the rest of his drink back and blurted out "Draya is pregnant."

With no hesitation I motioned to the bartender two more and took the seat next to his.

"Damn, Bro what the fuck?" I asked, as I sat my fitted on the bar stool beside me. I was mortified for Chris, he was a good dude, he is one of the first guys my age I met when we moved here. He was from the same hood as my cousin Brian, but that was about all they had in common. He did IT work for a firm by our building and was cool as hell. Once he worked his way out the hood, he didn't look back. Him and his girl Jae are a few years older than us and one of the few couples that we know that Lyne'e actually like spending time with. Shit Jae, is a few months pregnant herself.

"The fucked up part is I hadn't seen Draya sense we found out Jae was pregnant. I quit fucking with her, not even anything shady, just told her I was out. She said she was cool with it, shit after all she got a man, why would she trip on me?" he questioned, more to himself than to me. "Then out of nowhere yesterday I walked in the house to find the bitch was sitting in my kitchen. She told her, before she even told me about the baby. I mean who does that?" Another rhetorical question I'm sure.

I wanted to say something, but I didn't know what my words could do to ease the situation. I think I would shit a brick if I walked in my house to see Lyne'e and any bitch I was smashing sitting down talking. I gave the waitress my card and told her to keep them coming, it's obviously going to be a long night.

Chris continued "I didn't know what to say at first, I saw Draya sitting there and thought maybe they met in some fucked up twilight zone type of way, but when I saw the ultrasound picture on the table and the look on Jae's face I knew that was it. That bitch still never told me, she just got up grabbed her purse off my couch and walked out like a fucking fart in the wind."

"So how does she know it's yours?"

"The bitch don't, she gave Jae some story about not wanting to stress her out during this time, but couldn't sit by while I play fucking house and proud daddy to her baby while she has to do everything on her own. How her man left her when he found out about me and that was why I stopped fucking with her, but dawg, I swear it wasn't. I didn't know shit about her baby. Her and Draya are four weeks apart. What the fuck am I supposed to do with that?"

I sat silently, if there were words to impart on him I sure as shit didn't know them. Jae was cool as hell, she's really laid back and doesn't allow too much to bother her. Ever since they found out she was pregnant all Chris wanted to do is to be home with her. I've seen Draya, shit they met here at Bang, she was bad as fuck, 5'8", bright brown eyes, big ass and small everything else. She could easily be the baddie in a video or two. She had this cute little chunky face with dimples and a fade. Her line up was as tight as mine, but the shit looked good on her. We were all checking her out, but she had her eyes on Chris and didn't stop until she got him. As long as I've known him he was faithful, hell when I met him, they called him Church around his hood. No one knew about Draya but me, he knew if word got out then it was only a matter of time before Jae found out.

And he really tried not to hook up with her, but again Draya was bad as fuck, I don't know how he held out as long as he did. She just fell in this fool lap one day, but when he was done, he was done.

"So what now, are you going back home? Can you go back home?" I asked.

"She had my shit packed before I could say "let me explain", I'm telling you she was so mad. I've never seen her like that and I don't want to do anything to stress her out and it hurt the baby so I just left. I left without saying a word or sorry or anything. I knew that could only have made things worse and hurt more, but shit, what could I have said. I don't want her thinking I give a fuck about this girl, but I really didn't want to cause her more pain."

I requested the bill and told Chris he could stay at my place for a couple of days, it's not like Lyne'e was ever coming. Chris followed me home, swerving even though I didn't drive over thirty-five just to be safe. I got him set up in one of the other rooms downstairs and headed to my room to take a shower. My boy Chris was all fucked up, he was a good dude that made one mistake and it's going to possibly cost him everything. Not only does he stand to lose his girl but they share everything, he's going to lose that shit too.

The more I look at what Chris has going on the more I think Lyne'e is over reacting. Our shit it topical, there has never been a day where a bitch I was fucking with ever felt cool or mad enough to approach my woman and tell her shit. If Lyne'e wanted to be mad, she should look at this shit Jae had going on, pregnant and finding out that her man has someone else pregnant too. Now that's fucked up.

After my shower, I grabbed my phone to send one last text.

"... I'm sorry" A.Hobbs 12:23 am

Her Side... The Uncertainty

I woke up this morning to a text from Anderson. *"I'm sorry"* I wanted to reply, but I'm not ready to speak with him just yet. Besides what could he be sorry for, for popping up at my job, for hurting me, for calling me four times over four months, or for just being a fucking asshole? Either way, I'm not falling down this rabbit hole with him today. I have to go play nice with my parents for Paulette's birthday. The one day a year she is extra pissy just because she feels she can be. Usually she throws her bitter evilness around to prove a point, but on her birthday she spreads that shit like a whore spreads her legs at All-star weekend. From the moment she wakes up she is vicious, it usually starts with my dad for not getting her the gift she wants. Even though she makes him give her his credit card days in advance, so that she can buy exactly what she wants, he is usually an "inconsiderate asshole" because *he* didn't buy her something himself.

Then the venom is thrown on us, well me for ruining her perfect figure and indirectly her life. Of course she doesn't say any of this to us, it's usually on the phone to whatever idiot who choses to call and wish her a happy birthday. By the end of the day she has told at least two people that they need to stop eating, another that they can stand to get something nipped or tucked *unlike her which is all natural,* and has referred to three people as visually distracting and not in a good way. These days are always a delight because it's one of the few days that my father, Toni and I are all in agreement on putting her crazy ass in a nursing home as soon as we get the chance.

I could bribe Sloane and Keyla to come to the party with me, for some reason I was really in my feelings about Anderson, missing Jamal and just felt lonely.

"Thanks for coming today, I swear I do not have the energy to put up with Paulette's crazy today."

"No problem, I get it. You know I know all about crazy mothers. Or step mothers." Sloane mumbled staring out of the window.

"So what's going on with Jamal? Is he still here or coming back? Do you think you'll go visit him?" Keyla inquired.

"Nah, we agreed to let whatever this was between us happen in the moment and play it by ear."

"What's the problem? He's got good dick, a good job, good looks, smart and do I need to remind you, has good dick!" Keyla laughed. "Girl that man had you floating, OK? He was fucking you all over Illinois, had yo bougie ass walking around with no panties."

"And at work might I add." Sloane laughed.

Keyla continued "Please give me one good reason you can't make this work. And you better not say Anderson lame ass."

I was stuck; I knew there was an answer, but I had nothing. I didn't even turn to look in her direction, because I knew she was right. I just drove, quietly hoping that if I stated perfectly still all of the facts recently dropped would somehow not make sense.

"You know I'm right." She added. "Look, Lyne'e Anderson is great, I know you guys have a long history and deep down I think we all can agree he loves you. I know you two had a glorious future planned, but sometimes shit happens, and you have to make new plans. I'm always going to have your back and whatever decision you make I'll stand by it with you, but don't pass up a good thing for something familiar. Especially a familiar dick like Anderson lame ass."

"Preach" Sloane sang while throwing her hand in the air.

"You two don't get it." I murmured, trying my hardest not to let the floodgates open. "Yes, Anderson is an asshole, but what we had was more than just time invested. Our lives were intertwined in some of the most amazing ways. You have no idea how it feels to have someone who has you, that knows the ugliest parts of you and still has you. And still want you. This job bullshit was one thing, but until this happened, we really didn't have any real big issue. Yeah, I thought he was fucking with someone else at some point, but I didn't really have any proof, as far as I know I was in my own head. I wasn't finding numbers in his phone or hoes weren't coming to the house. He wasn't putting his hands on me, we just hit a wall. Hard. It was more than just familiarity or good dick it was all the things that make two people actually love."

I found myself just staring out the window hoping that no one saw me cry. We pulled up at my parent's house just as the decorators were leaving, my daddy arranged for Paulette to have a full Elizabethan masquerade ball for her birthday party. He had the backyard decorated with two thrones, hired jesters & jugglers, requested everyone dress the part, hell he even had portraits of her in every corner. Even with all the party treating her like royalty she still found a way to complain about something.

I stood on the side and listened to her complain that the live band was too loud and she couldn't hear herself think. My poor dad, he has always just taken it, all of her ungrateful, unappreciative, self-centered bullshit, he just accepted. I have always been in awe of his patients. I grabbed my glass of wine and an extra bottle I stashed by my purse and headed to the front porch. I really couldn't take anymore of my mother and just needed some air. The last time I snuck away from a party here, it was my going away party, my life couldn't be any more different today than it was then.

"Hey beautiful!"

I looked up the moment I heard his voice; it was Anderson slowly walking towards me. *What could he be doing here?* "Hello, sir."

He sat down next to me and rocked close enough to nudge my shoulder with his. "She can't be that bad already that you had to escape."

"Ha, you know Paulette, even when the show is all about her, it's still not good enough." I laughed as I finished the last of my wine. "So what are you doing here?" I asked.

"Your dad invited me, is that a problem?"

I wanted to tell him yes, ask him to leave because the smell of his cologne and the feel of his shoulder on mine is distracting me from my well-earned anger.

"Nah you're good, but you should go dance for the queen before she sends for your head."

"I will, don't leave while I'm back there. You know I know where you live!" he joked before getting up.

Anderson's showing up was exactly the problem, we knew each other; we are connected in a way that I don't think I want to be connected to another person. He knows all of my shit and I his; we have invested everything in one another. We are who we are because of each other, well maybe more so him. I don't know if I'm ready to let that go just for good dick.

I spent the rest of the night walking up and down my childhood street talking and laughing with Anderson as if we had just met. He told me about Irwin and how things were going and I told him about my job. He caught me up on Chris and Jae's messy affair and I told him about running into Da'vere and some Philippine woman in the nail shop. We laughed until our cheeks were sore and then we laughed some more. The night may have been to celebrate the monster that I have to call mother, but it turned out to be one of the best evenings Anderson and I had in years.

His Side... The Healing

Tonight reminded me of the old Anderson and Lyne'e. I can't think of a single person I can laugh and be my myself with like I am with her.

"So can I ask you a question and it not ruin our evening?"

"It depends." She smiled graciously in my direction.

"Are you seeing anyone? Like for real?" I asked, knowing I don't think I'm really ready for the answer.

I watched as those big eyes of hers filled with wonder and searched the night sky for the right answer.

"I am not." She finally answered. "What about you?" She questioned, bumping her soft hip into mine.

"Nah. I'd be lying if I told you I didn't try, but the truth is, all I want is you." For a moment our steps slowed down and the only sound to be heard were the white noise of Chicago nights.

"Hmmm" She sighed.

"Hmmm what?" I asked.

"Nah, it's crazy. When I was there, you didn't seem to have any time or interest in me. Now all you want is me. Just strange, that's all."

"I know, but it doesn't change how I feel. What's that saying, you don't know what you have until it's gone."

"Hmmm."

The rest of the walk back home was quiet and slow. I tried to fill the silence by swatting at flies or mosquitos crossing our path, hoping that I look silly enough to provoke a laugh or protective enough to spark up a new line of conversation. Unfortunately, she didn't take the bait. By the time we reached her parents' front porch we were all out of things to say.

Just in time to put an end to our uncomfortable silence, Keyla and Sloane came walking out of the front door with plates in their hands and a bottle of wine peeking out of Keyla's purse.

"Hey, so it looks like the party is over but my homeboy has us on the list at this spot I know, you coming?" Keyla asked Lyne'e as she stepped off the porch.

"Nah I think I'm going to go home and get some rest."

"No, don't be like that, come out with us." Sloane intervened.

"You know how I am after spending the day with Paulette, honestly I just want to go to sleep."

"Okay, so what are you going to do, ride home with Anderson? Are we taking you home first? What do you want?" Sloane asked, as she stepped in front of me like I wasn't even there to check on Lyne'e.

"It's no big deal I'm sure I can have somebody here give me a ride home."

"I can take you home." I stepped in.

"No, I don't want you to have to go out of your way."

"You know it's no problem, let me go say goodnight to your mother and if you're ready, we can go."

"Are you sure?" she asked.

"I promise it's fine. Let me make sure you get home, please?" I watched as the uncomfortable smile on her face softened and she nodded her head in agreement. Standing next to two very different, very beautiful women she's still the most amazing thing I've ever laid eyes on. Right now she's hurting and I get it. It's probably my fault, but I'll wait and give her the time she needs to realize that she and I are always going to be together.

After we said our goodnights to everybody, she and I walked to my car. It's funny she knows me better than anyone yet I'm nervous. I felt like we were on a first date. I felt jittery. Even she looked uncomfortable as I opened the door for her. It's been so long since she and I have been in the same space, let alone the same vehicle, so much has changed since riding around in our little red shooter. I whip through the streets of Chicago dipping in and out of traffic playing sounds from a mix CD that she left at the house. I turned the air off and let the windows down so that the night air can wash over us and hopefully break the tension in the car. Right when everything was going smoothly my phone rang. I can literally hear her rolling her eyes as I reached down to grab it. I'm sure she thinks it's some female calling, but I was more than thrilled to wipe that look off her face and show her the caller I.D. It was actually my mom probably calling to see how the party went since it was her idea that I go.

"Hey Momma" I answered.

Hey little bro, you got a second?"

"Yeah, why you calling from Momma's phone, what's wrong?"

"Where you at?" He asked?

"I'm driving, why?"

"We need to talk." He demanded.

"Yo Will, what the fuck is going on, where is my Momma and why are you calling me from her phone?" I scolded. I pay my parent's phone bills to help them out, not so that Will can avoid yet another bill.

"Pops is in the hospital. I think you should get here." The second the words hit my ears I felt something cold and numbing surge through me. I don't even remember breathing, just the lights from the cars flickering in front of me.

"Give me the wheel. Let it go Anderson please." Lyne'e cried out. "Fuck, slow down, Anderson, come on slow down, you're going to kill us. Stop."

The moment I regained awareness, I could see Lyne'e holding the steering wheel and hear her yelling for me to break. I feel like I blinked and everything around me had changed again.

"We will be there as soon as possible. Ok, ok, see you soon." Lyne'e said on my phone.

I don't even remember her taking the phone from me. "Is my pops dead?" I cried. She didn't need to answer me, the tears in her eyes said it loud enough for me. "Come on, let me drive." She demanded as she opened her car door and hoped out. I watched as she walked in front of the car and over to my side. She let herself in and without missing a beat she pulled me into her arms and let me fall apart.

"I know, baby I'm so sorry." She whispered as she cried with me.

We sat on the side of the road, for what felt like hours as I cried over the loss of my dad. I don't even remember when I fell asleep, but when I woke up, we were about an hour out from my mom's house.

The time blaring on the dashboard was 2:34 am and Lyne'e was singing along to the cd still playing that I had put in hours ago. I didn't say a word, and neither did she. She gave me a half smile and continued to sing. For the rest of the ride I think I had just about every thought or memory of my dad running through my mind. His unsolicited life advice, his unwarranted lectures, his hands, his hugs, his tips on how to be a man. All of it. The amount of love that man has for all of us, gone.

We pulled up at my parent's house and sat there for a second.

"Go ahead, I'll be right in, let me call my dad and let him know we made it." Lyne'e requested with a smile.

When I walked in the house, my Momma was sitting at the dining room table staring at my dad's favorite hat. Her usually joyful eyes were now the saddest shade of brown I've ever seen. Although it was almost four in the morning, all the lights were on, the kids were all awake and my siblings were all there moving around doing something. The house still smelled like my dad, strangely I can still feel his presence although the hurt in my mom's eyes makes it all too clear he is gone. I walked right past everyone and fell to my knees at my mom's lap. The second she wrapped me in her arms I felt like something inside of me had broken. I cried in her arms like a baby, she held me tighter with every shiver. I wasn't just hurt because I lost my father, my mother lost the love of her life. Her protector, her rock. I can't remember a day that these two weren't in love, or touching on one another. He used to joke that one day I'd find a woman half as amazing as my mother, and now she has to go on without him.

"Come on in, baby." My mom cried. "Thank you for bringing my baby here safely."

I look over and realize she was speaking to Lyne'e. Until this moment it didn't register that she drove me to another state without fail or hesitation to be with my family. I watched as she and my family grieved over my father. I watched as my love for her grew more than I could have ever imagined.

I CAN'T REMEMBER THE last time I spent this much time with my family, but I think two weeks is my limit. Liv and Ash have their own places and Will stays at his girl's spot so I thought it was going to be just me and my momma, but damn I was wrong. She insisted that we all stay together a couple of nights, and it was fun at first then I remembered how much I loved living alone. I like quiet and order, my family thrive in chaos and clutter. I couldn't believe how soft my mom had gotten, if we ran through her house the way my nieces and nephews did we'd still be picking her foot out our ass's. And Will's kids were the worst. He was nothing like our dad, there was no popping, thumbing or snatching them up, just yelling. The worst part was the yelling was a joke because the kids never stopped. That house was barely big enough for the six of us back in the day, I don't know what my mom was thinking about adding seven more.

The upside is I'm no longer the baby brother they all get to pick on and make do shit. My sisters stopped being able to beat me decades ago and Will is always drunk, I'm pretty sure I could level this house without breaking a sweat. They traded in calling me a Momma's Boy to calling me boogie. I didn't eat all the crap they ate, so that meant I thought I was better than them. I wasn't sleeping on the couch, so I forgot where I came from. I would wake up and go for a run, that meant I was showing off. And every time I made fun of how fat and sloppy all of them were I got in trouble. Momma didn't hear any of the shit they were saying to me, she only heard me. I guess some shit never changes.

Once Momma finally had her share of family time and sent them bad ass kids back home, I was able to help her get everything in order. My dad had most things prepared in case of his death, but my mom still needed someone to walk her through transferring things to her name. My sisters are barely managing their own lives and Will's dumb ass can't tie his shoes without direction. They paid the cars and house off; I made sure my parent's money was good years ago. Against my wishes, my mom gave dad's car to Will, and he left us all a little money. I sat the grandkids up to get theirs when they turn eighteen and this way the little my dad had to share would grow into something real. My siblings could fuck off their funds however they want, but I want the next generation to have a fighting chance. Before leaving, I paid to have the security on the house updated since she insisted on staying here and I bought her a small handgun to keep in the house. Most of the neighbors know my parents and I'm sure they will look out for her, but I want her to be as safe and protected as possible.

The moment I stepped into my house I could run and kiss everything. Usually I hate this quiet, but today. Today is not one of those days. I dropped my bags at the door and two stepped to the kitchen. I grabbed a small glass, some ice and my favorite small batch of whiskey that I had hid at the back of the bar. Chris was gone back home, Jae came to my dad's services, and they talked there. I'm sure he'll tell me how it happened, but for now I'm just glad to have my house back.

Work on the other hand was a fucking shitshow. Someone had moved most of my accounts to other people as if I was never coming back and the big ones all went to one person. That fucking whore Teagan. Companies that I brought on, companies that I grew, people that I facilitated relationships with, all gone. I skipped right past my supervisor Lockhorn and went straight to Irwin's office. I know he's the only person who would have given my shit to this bitch.

"Irwin, you've got a second?" I asked, walking past Gracie, his gatekeeper.

"Yeah, sure son come on in. I'm so sorry to hear about your father, I know how much he meant to you." He replied, while waving his hand at Gracie who was standing there furious at my maneuver. "Tell me how your family is holding up? And your mom, she is such a sweet lady."

Put off by his approach, and a little distracted. I felt my brows and forehead relax a little as I made my way towards the hand that he was holding out for me. The moment I went in to shake it he pulled me in for a hug. Irwin is a man that I respect, look up to professionally even. Though in all of my years working here, I don't ever think I've seen him show any authentic emotion or compassion towards anyone. In a million years I never would have thought I'd be the person he showed it too. I didn't make a habit of hugging anyone really, my dad, my brother, or maybe Mr. Riggs, but that was about all. Until I got the call about my dad, I couldn't even remember the last time I cried about something. Yet here I am, a grown ass man, standing in my boss's executive suit trying not to break down.

"Yeah, I still can't believe that I won't pick up the phone and hear his voice anymore." I paused, thinking about the last conversation he and I had. "He was a real man and an amazing dad. Even when he didn't have it, he always made a way to get it. I hope to be half the man he was one day."

"You're well on your way." He expressed, as he walked back behind his desk. "So what is it I can do for you?"

"Oh yeah, my accounts. Do you know who reassigned all of my accounts to Teagan and why?"

"Yes, we figured you would use more time to handle your father's affairs, and she offered to help manage your clients."

Judging by the look on his whipped face, I couldn't determine if he really thought this was a good ideal or if he had no clue how manipulative his fuck buddy was.

"Sir. I'm fine. I appreciate Teagan's attempt at altruism, but I'm good. I do not need help with my clients. Nia was kind enough to reschedule my appointments for next week and those clients that were inconvenienced, quickly sent their remorse and some even cards and flowers. I think Teagan may be great at a lot of things, but since joining the company she has gone above and beyond to alienate herself from team functions. She does not know how to work with a team and she is incredibly rude to almost everyone she comes in contact with. Well, with the exception of you." I advised while adjusting in my seat. "I mean this in the most transparent way possible, if the life line being offered comes from her, I do not want it. She shows no compunction for her actions and while others may be too afraid to ruffle any feathers and say anything I am not."

I waited for Irwin to blow a gasket or to flip out, but much to my surprise he kept his cool. Probably because any loud noise in Teagan's direction could mean extra fuel to their little fire.

"I understand, I'll make sure she has turned over all notes on your files after our meeting this morning."

"Thank you, sir. I really appreciate you taking care of this."

I stepped off the elevator just as Teagan and her office flunky Rody were waiting to get on. She smirked in my direction as they walked past me, never interrupting her conversation. I find it quite interesting that someone so worried about my well being didn't open her mouth to offer an actual ounce of a fuck about what I had going on. Instead of returning the gesture, I stepped past them both as if they were never in my way.

"Knock, Knock."

"Hey, come on in." Nia waved as she saw my head peak through her door. "I can't believe your back so soon." She smiled as she jumped up to hug me. Nia is without a doubt my work wife. She's one of the coolest women I've ever met and if she wasn't already married to a marine, I'd definitely would've pressed her.

"I feel like I owe you lunch, so tell me what you want and I will run out and get it." I said giving her the friendliest church hug I could. I like her husband, but I'm pretty sure most of his kills were for fun.

"Please, I had to go toe to toe with Horney Bear, you owe me coffee and lunch!"

"Bet, I can use one too."

While we walked down the street to the coffee shop, she caught me up on everything I missed while I was gone. That was the thing about Nia, she reminded me so much of Lyne'e. She always spoke her mind, she rarely apologize for any of it, and although it may have been blunt, it was always honest. If she said, she saw Teagan snooping through my office, then she saw her.

"I just can't believe they let her have access to my shit, without so much of a courtesy call or email." I complained, as the barista gave me my cup.

"Right. So when you saw her this morning did you tell her?"

"Nope, I'd rather see her face when it comes from Irwin. I hope his ass do it in the meeting." We both laughed.

We gathered in the conference room and listened to Fred Gilbran, the company's CFO rave about our quarterly numbers. Then to Irwin as he explained the importance of working as a team and being kind to one another. Finally, ending his kumbaya speech by pointing out the potential for growth if we all worked as one, before asking if anyone had questions. I could barely keep my cool as I watched people preparing to leave the room, Teagan included and not one word about my accounts.

A million thoughts rushed through my head including my new mortgage, if I reacted the way I wanted to. There is no way I was going to let these two fuck me out of all that I had built.

"Anderson, one moment do you have a second?" Irwin asked while everyone was gathering their things.

"Actually, I am on my way to meet with HR, can it wait?" I lied, before shifting my eyes over to Teagan.

The entire look on Irwin's face had changed, it was as if all the blood had left his face and the ghost of my ancestors was standing before him.

"Um, well one moment." He murmured to the room. "First, I want to welcome Anderson back and again give my condolences to you and your family. Also, it has been brought to my attention that we have teammates overstepping and undercutting one another. That is not how we do business in house here at BDI. I do not understand why any of Anderson's accounts have been reassigned, but if you have a newly assigned account that belongs to him, please cease any communication with his clients and send him your notes. Please make sure he has them by the end of the day."

Not a single person opened their mouth, everyone looked around the room in confusion and whispered amongst themselves or smiled at me.

"Oh, I'll be more specific for you, sir. Teagan, I believe only you have my accounts. Apparently you were in my office while I was away and going through my things." I announced.

"What, wait, no. I was trying to help you. Rearranging your schedule while you were out. Making sure you clients had everything they needed at the end of the month. I understand how stressful losing a parent is, and I wanted to help you in any way I could. Honestly, I thought I was being a team player." She said to everyone in the room, but me.

"It sounds like an honest mistake and an overreaction to me Anderson." Carol added from across the room. I can't stand her ass either.

"Really, that would have been a gracious gesture to show concern for me while I was going through such a difficult time, especially had you taken the time to actually call or ask me what I needed help with. You know like Nia did, when she offered to reschedule my meetings. Or if maybe when you saw me this morning, had you spoken to me before brushing past me to go get your coffee? I don't know, maybe then I would have seen it as you offering an act of kindness, but a person who has my office unlocked the day after I take my leave and doesn't even bother to speak to me, doesn't come off like a friend or a teammate."

I watched as the sea of blue and green eyes that were previously staring at me with judgment and contempt were now fixated on her or looking at the ground.

"Anderson, that's not fair." Teagan replied, tears beginning to form in the corners of her eyes.

"Hmm, well fair and truthful are often two different things. I have a client coming in this afternoon, if you could get my accounts back to me, that would be great." I asked, before taking my leave. They will paint me as the bad guy if I stay any longer.

I spent the rest of my day getting my business affairs back in line and receiving strange looks from every fair-complected employee in the building. It's crazy how I can be the bad guy for standing up for myself and the fucking villan is now the victim.

Her Side ... The Knowing

I agreed to meet him for lunch today, but I must have made a wrong turn, because I'm in some sort of residential area. Granted the houses were big and beautiful, but there is nowhere to have lunch around here. Just as I was getting ready to drive back to the main road I spotted the address and saw Anderson's car parked outside. I pulled into the driveway and noticed the baby bed box.

I turned off my car and reluctantly stepped out; I surveyed the street before realizing this is the same address he asked me to come to before. I rang the doorbell and was surprised to see Anderson in a bath towel answering the door. He flashed that big beautiful smile and invited me inside of the house. *Is this his new place, did he invite me here to gloat or be funny?*

"Come in, give me one second, I just got in and wanted to take a quick shower before you got here. Make yourself at home and I'll be right back." He said as he hurried off somewhere in the house. I looked around and there were no pictures, no bills or magazines to give me some sort of clue as to whose house this was. Through the kitchen window I could see that baby crib box and suddenly I could feel my heart falling to the floor. *Is this him and someone else's place? Is it his place, and he now has a baby on the way? Is that what this is about, he wants to tell me to my face, he doesn't want to be caught out there like Chris. Is that why he told me about Chris?*

Anderson came down the stairs and met me in the kitchen. "Let me get you something to drink. How was the traffic?"

"Traffic? Anderson, whose house am I standing in?" I snapped. I really tried not to, but if he was about to tell me he had a baby on the way, I needed to already be in the right mindset.

The smirk that slowly spread across his face only made me angrier. He is so fucking arrogant, and that smirk reminds me of how he played me. I stood with my arms folded waiting for an answer, but he never said a word. Instead, he opened the refrigerator, grabbed two Corona's with one hand and grabbed my hand with the other and led me out of the kitchen and to the stairs. He walked me up the stairs while insisting that I calm down and wait.

The stairs curved once we made it to the top landing, and I counted four doors and another set of stairs. All the doors were closed but one, and that was the room we walked into. I noticed the walls were all freshly painted, and I saw the baby crib in the corner. This was it, I felt sick to my stomach. If this man brought me here to meet the bastard kid he had while we were together I'm going to kill him and splatter his blood on these pretty walls. My heart was racing, and I was shocked silent, he took my hand in his and looked me in the eyes as he told me how much he loved me. *Love will not stop me from murdering you.*

He walked us over to the baby bed, inside was a small black box. I think my racing heart stopped as I focused on the open box and ring inside. It was the same ring that I gave him when I left, but it seemed bigger. He didn't get down on one knee; he held my hand in his and promised to be better, promised to do better. He promised to be whatever man it was that I needed as long as I promised to marry him. He explained that he bought the house a month ago and all he wanted was to fill it with me and our children. He swore he wasn't going anywhere and would wait for me to come around, if that was what it took and how nothing before this day mattered. He promised that we are on the same path and I was right, that he should have fought harder for us, and that it should not have taken him so long to realize what he had in me, and for that he was truly, deeply sorry. There was nothing I could do to stop the tears from falling, I don't know if it was him admitting to all the things that I already knew, or the fact that he finally figured it out.

Maybe it was the grand gesture. The house, the ring, the baby bed. We were married eight months later.